Dear Parent:

Psst . . . you're looking at the Super Secret Weapon of Reading. It's called comics.

STEP INTO READING® COMIC READERS are a perfect step in learning to read. They provide visual cues to the meaning of words and helpfully break out short pieces of dialogue into speech balloons.

Here are some terms commonly associated with comics:

PANEL: A section of a comic with a box drawn around it.
CAPTION: Narration that helps set the scene.
SPEECH BALLOON: A bubble containing dialogue.
GUTTER: The space between panels.

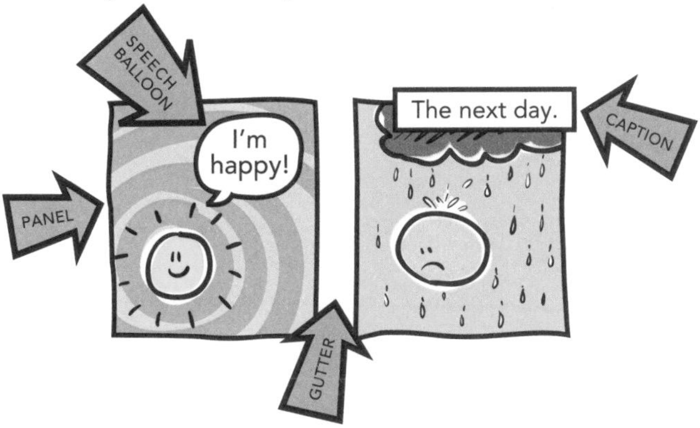
SPEECH BALLOON
I'm happy!
PANEL
The next day.
CAPTION
GUTTER

Tips for reading comics with your child:

- **Have your child read the speech balloons while you read the captions.**
- **Ask your child: What is a character feeling? How can you tell?**
- **Have your child draw a comic showing what happens after the book is finished.**

STEP INTO READING® COMIC READERS are designed to engage and to provide an empowering reading experience. They are also fun. The best-kept secret of comics is that they create lifelong readers. ***And that will make you the real hero of the story!***

M.HOLM

Jennifer L. Holm and Matthew Holm
Co-creators of the Babymouse and Squish series

To Mr. Dinko.
Thank you!
—T.C.

Visit us on the Web!
rhcbooks.com

Educators and librarians, for a variety of teaching tools, visit us at RHTeachersLibrarians.com

Library of Congress Cataloging-in-Publication Data
Name: Cummings, Troy, author.
Title: Arfy and the stinky smell / by Troy Cummings.
Description: First edition. | New York : Random House Children's Books, [2023] |
Series: Step into reading | Audience: Ages 4–6. |
Summary: "Arfy wants to prove just how good he is at smelling by tracking down the stinky smell going through his neighborhood." —Provided by publisher.
Identifiers: LCCN 2022027826 (print) | LCCN 2022027827 (ebook) |
ISBN 978-0-593-64370-9 (trade) | ISBN 978-0-593-64371-6 (lib. bdg.) |
ISBN 978-0-593-64372-3 (ebook)
Subjects: CYAC: Dogs—Fiction. | Smell—Fiction. | LCGFT: Animal fiction. |
Picture books.
Classification: LCC PZ7.C91494 Ar 2023 (print) | LCC PZ7.C91494 (ebook) |
DDC [E]—dc23

Printed in the United States of America
10 9 8 7 6 5 4 3 2 1

First Edition

This book has been officially leveled by using the F&P Text Level Gradient™ Leveling System.

A COMIC READER

STEP INTO READING®

STEP 2

ARFY AND THE STINKY SMELL

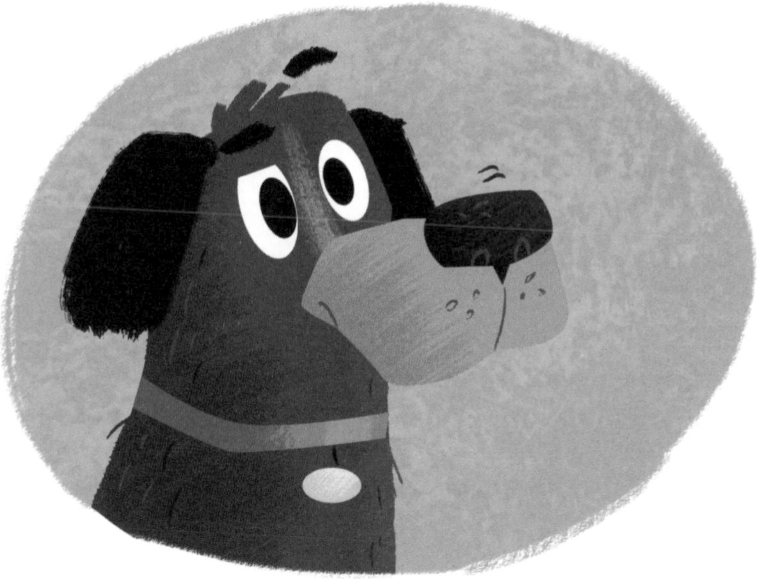

by Troy Cummings

Random House New York

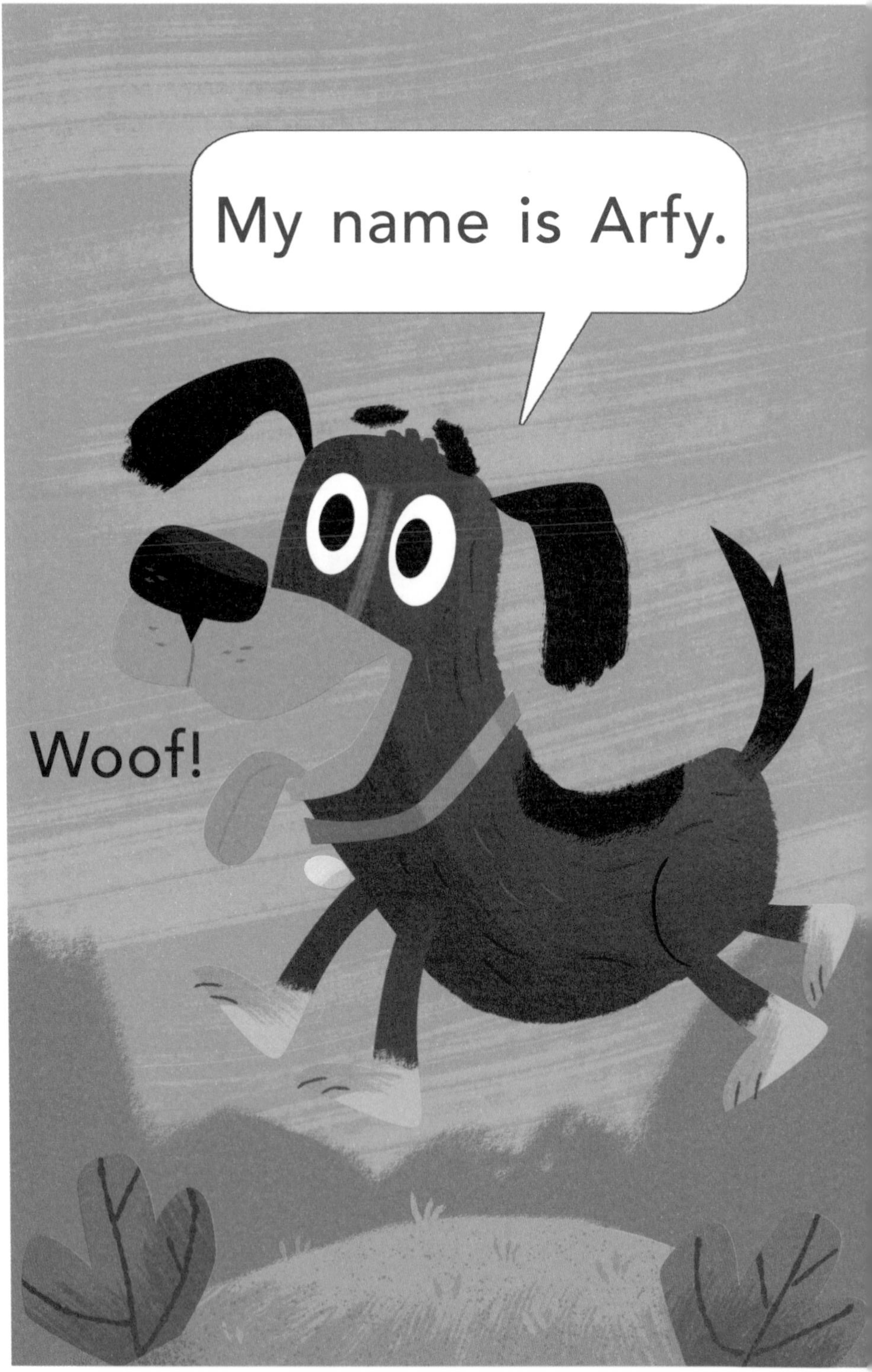
My name is Arfy.
Woof!

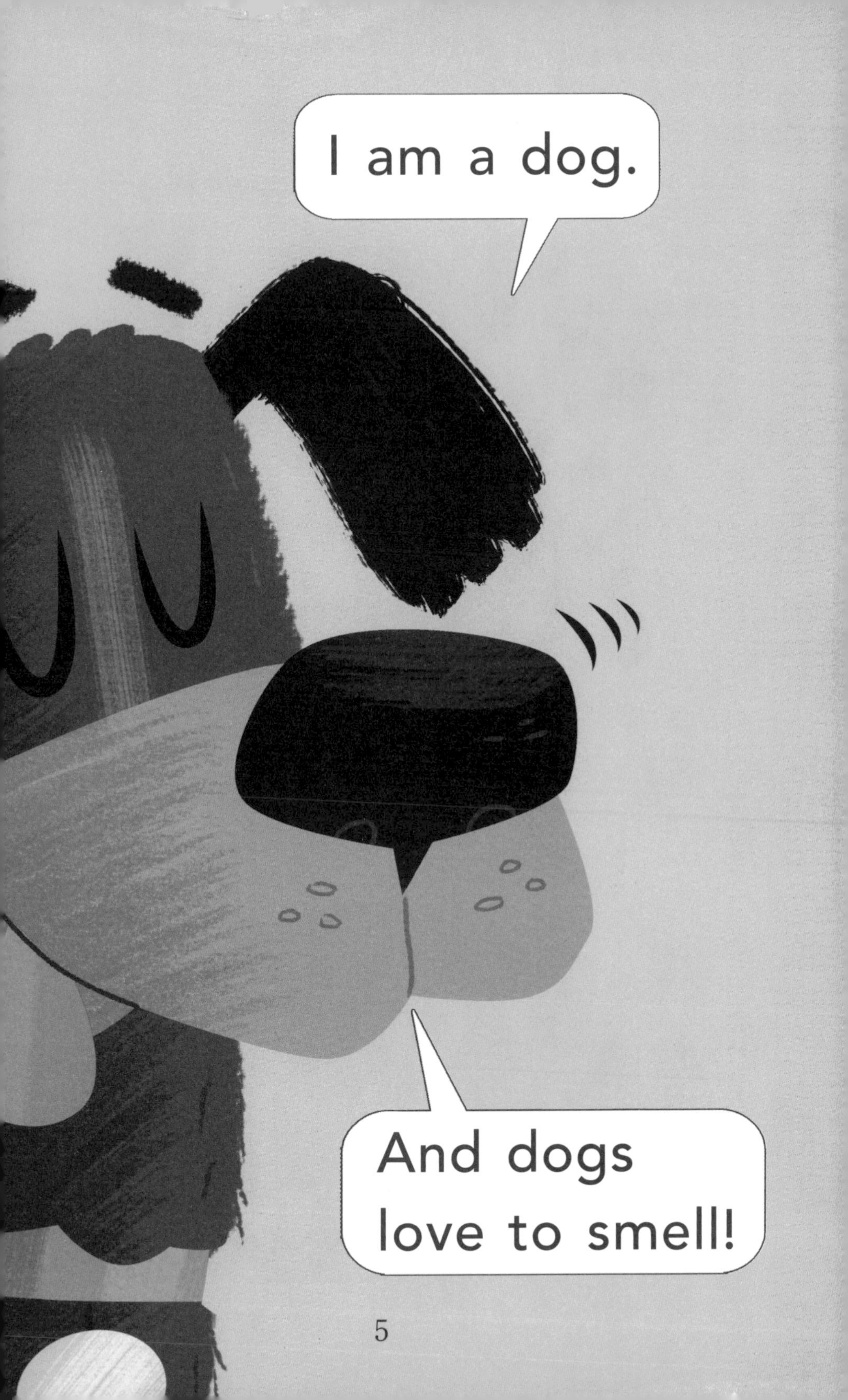
I am a dog.
And dogs love to smell!

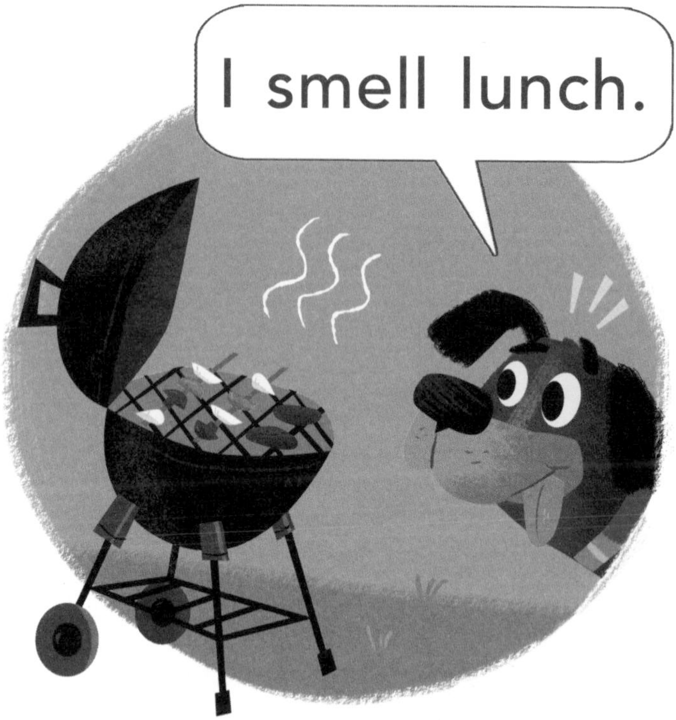
I smell lunch.

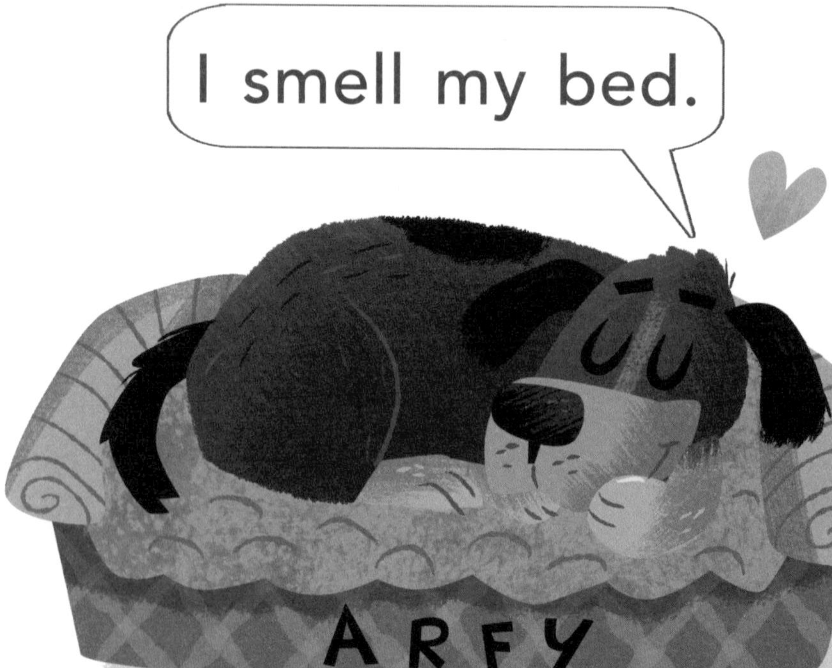
I smell my bed.
ARFY

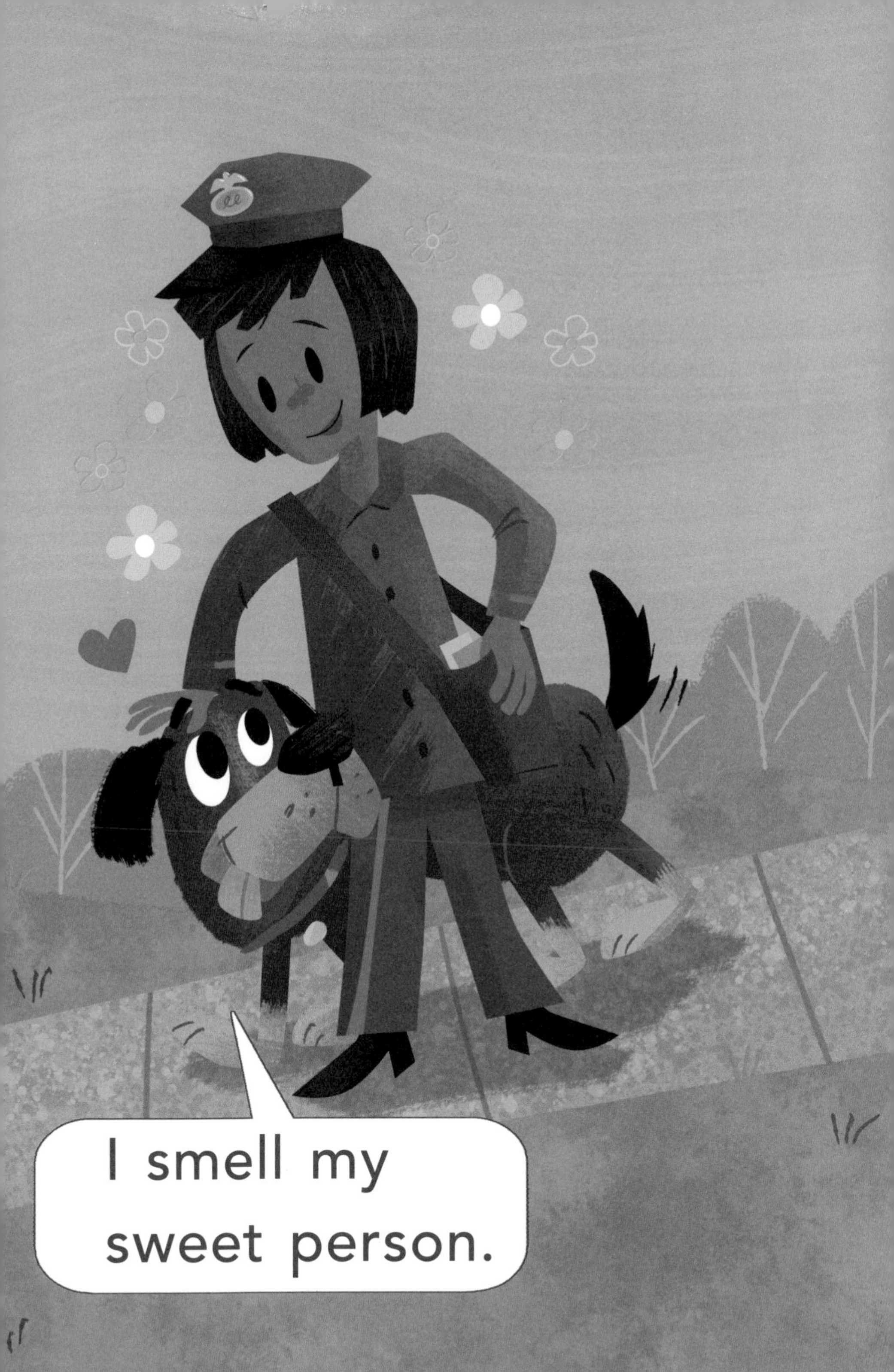
I smell my sweet person.

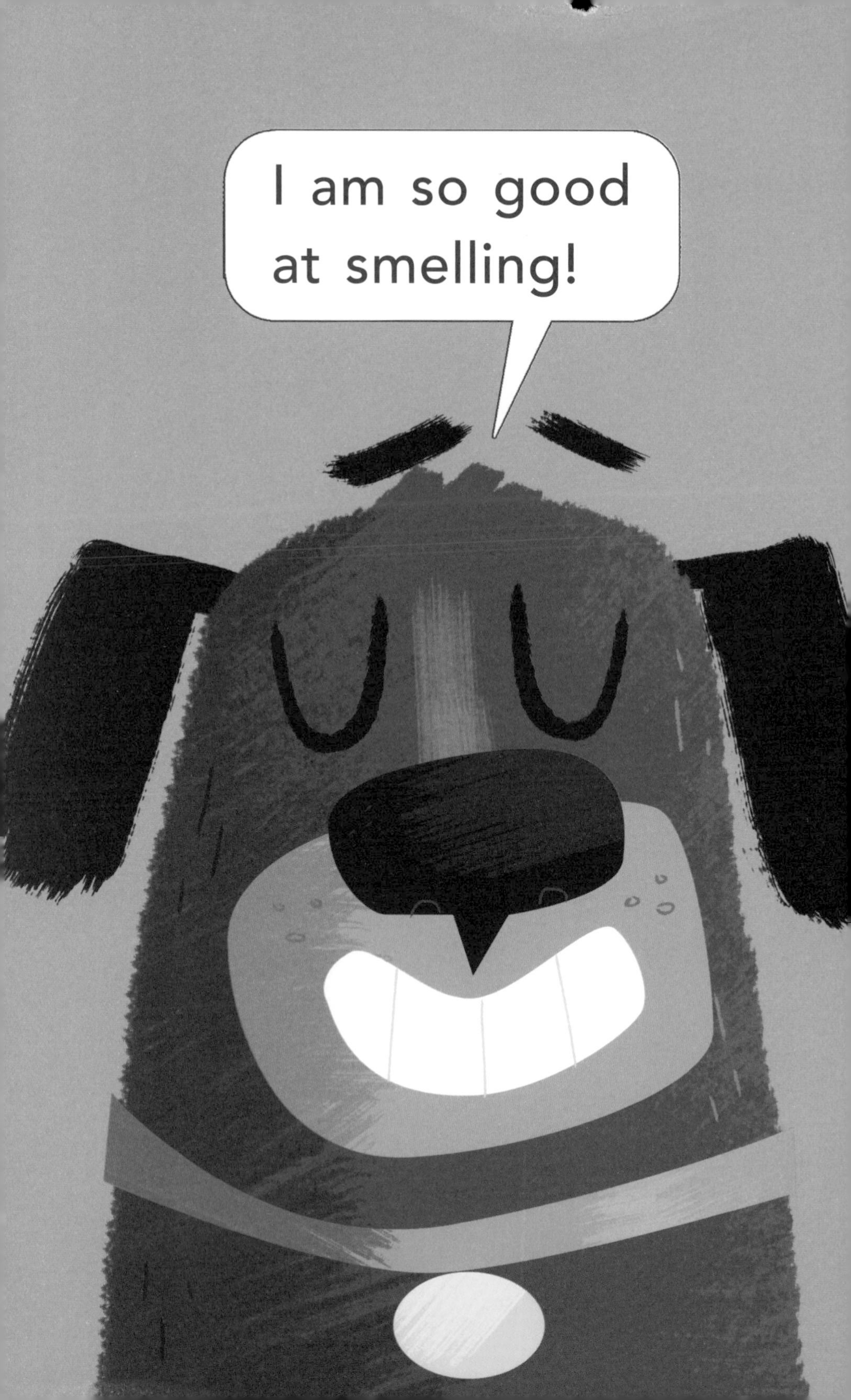
I am so good at smelling!

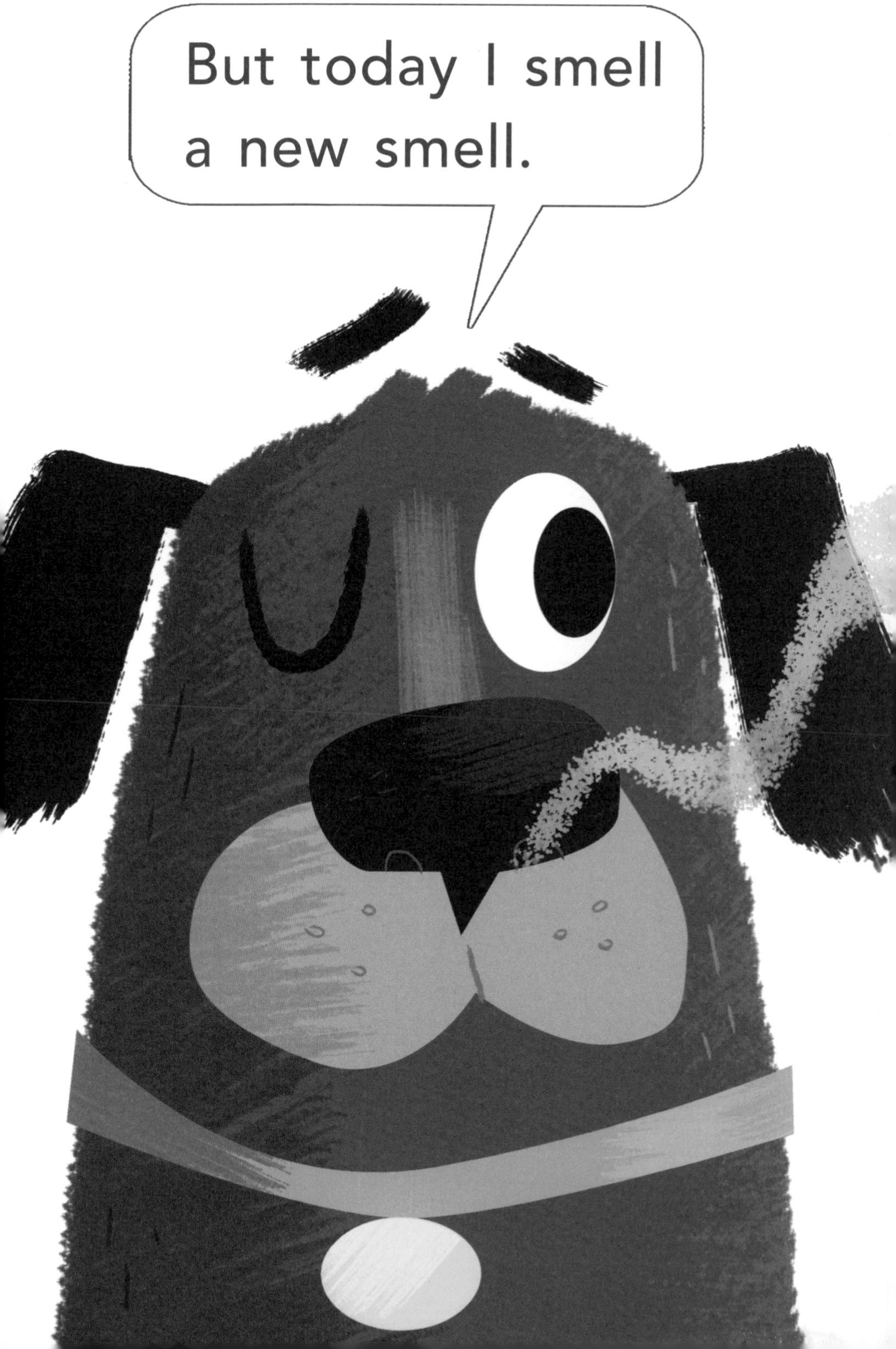
But today I smell a new smell.

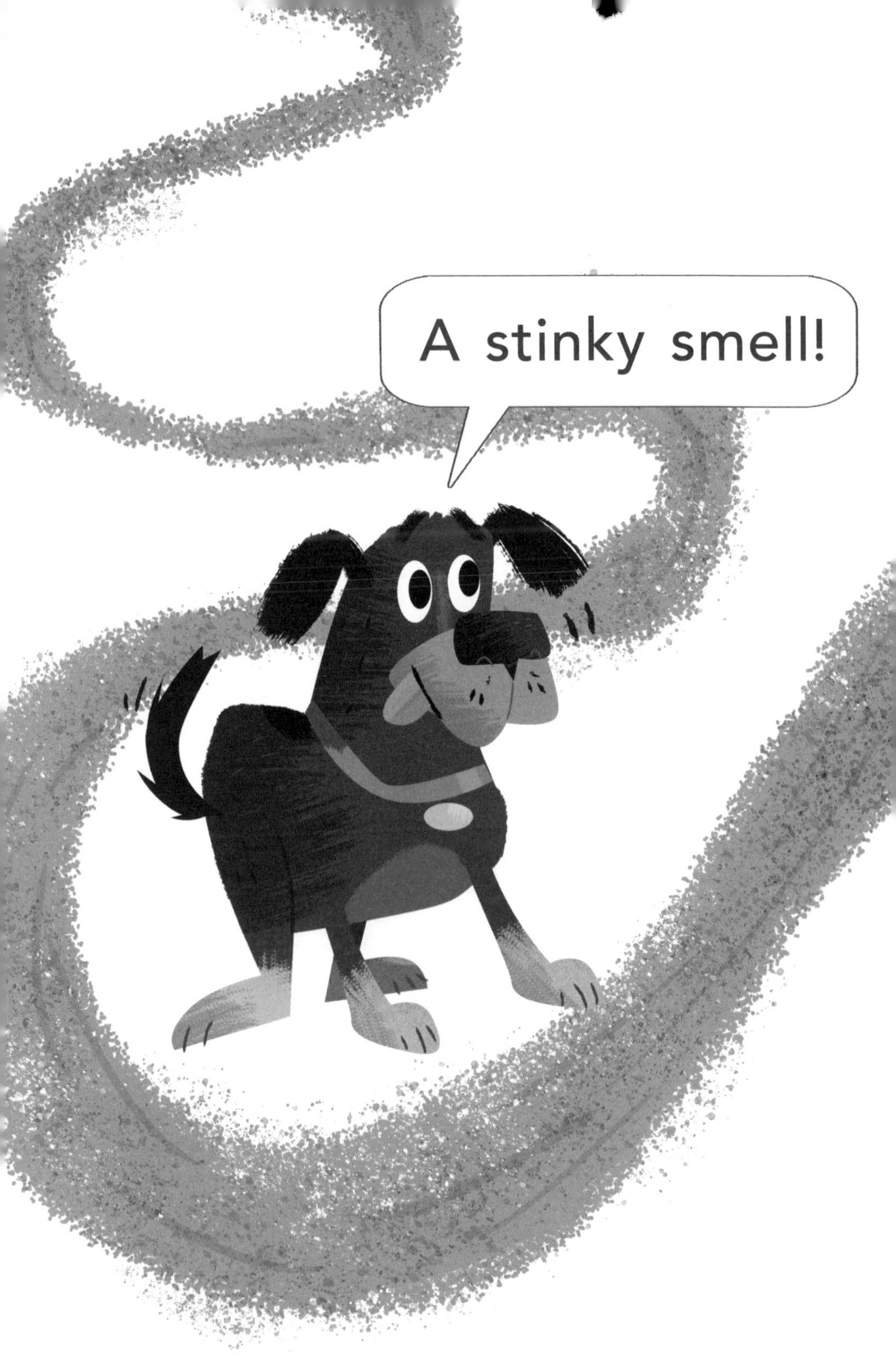
A stinky smell!

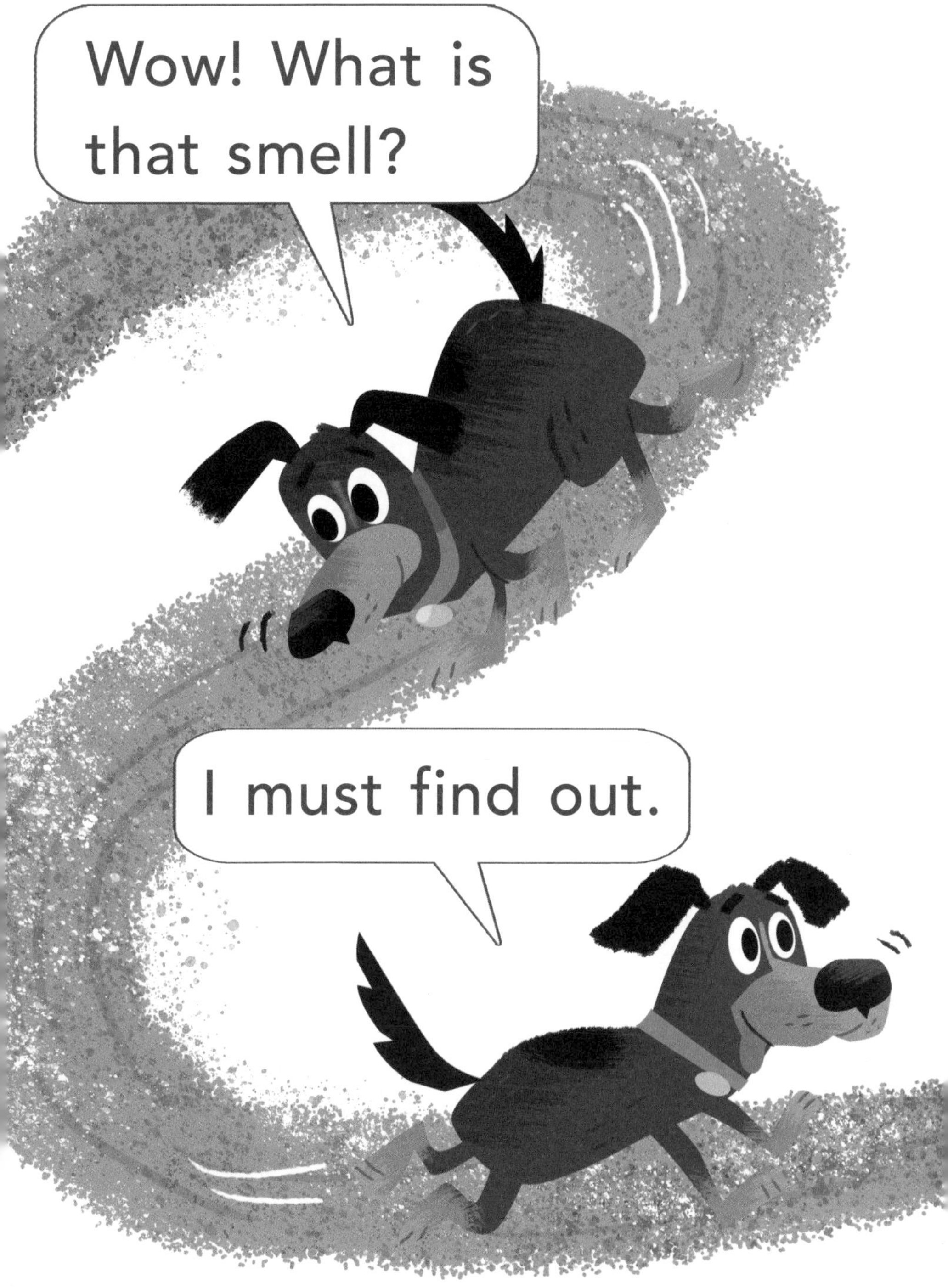
Wow! What is that smell?
I must find out.

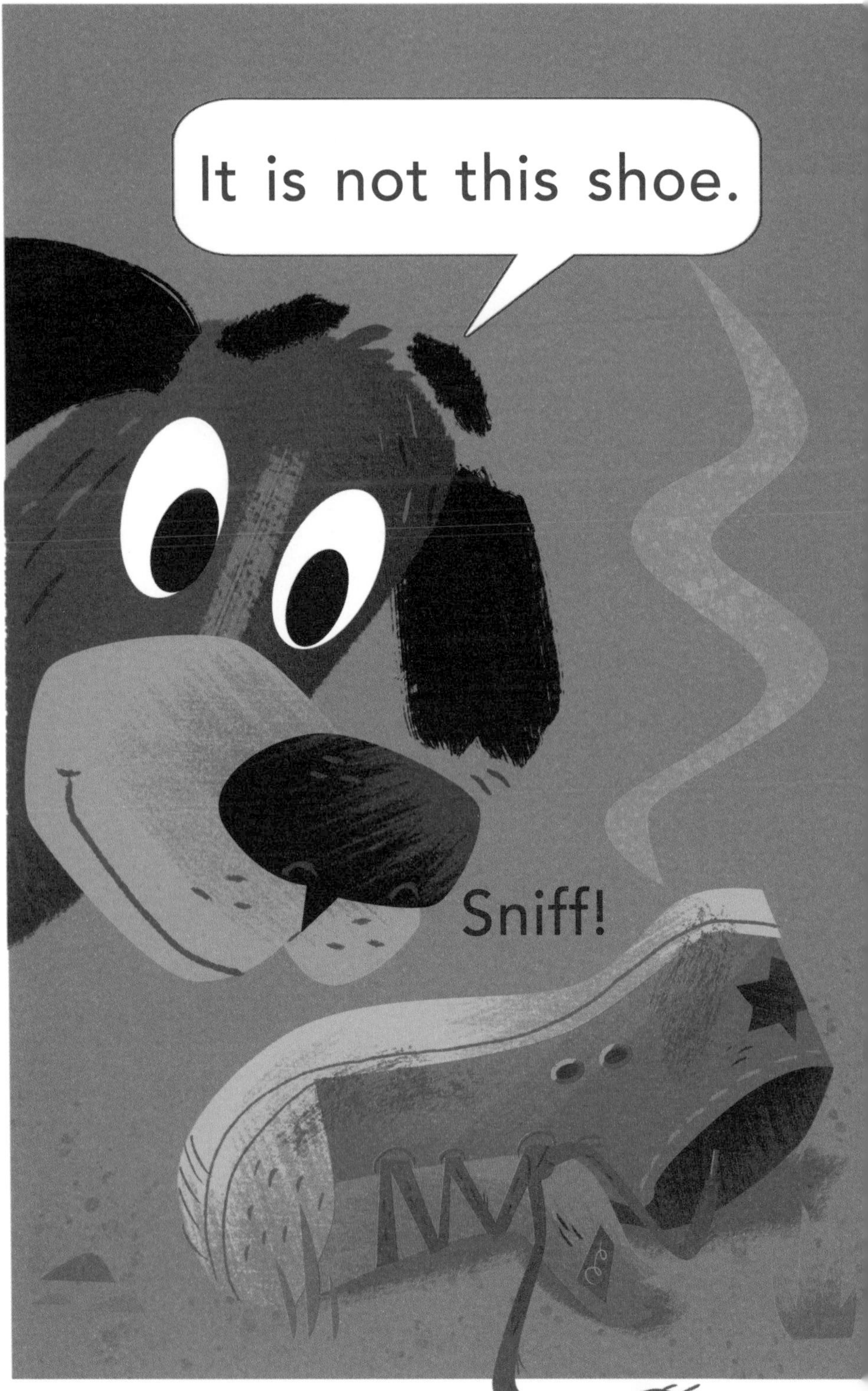
It is not this shoe.
Sniff!

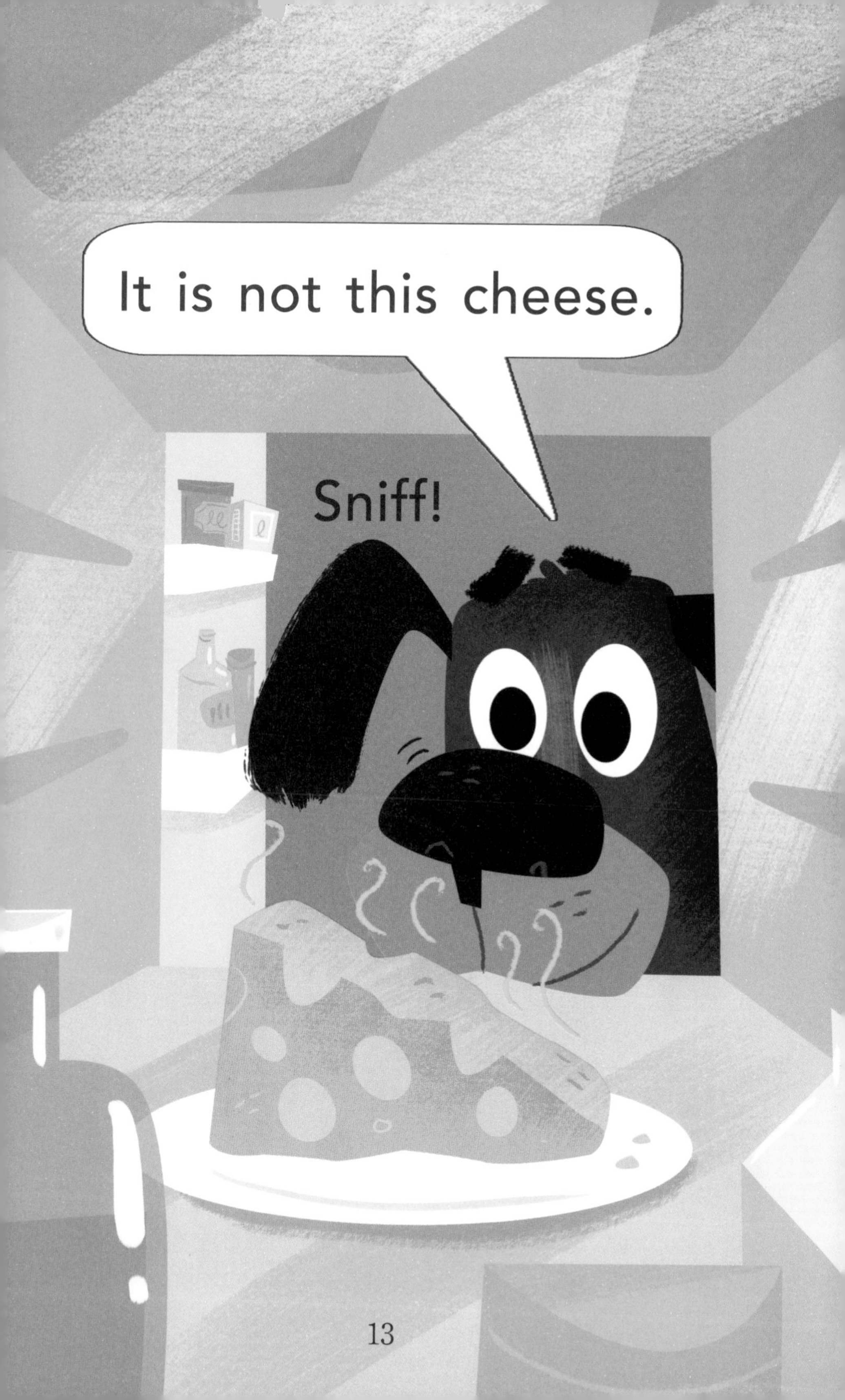
It is not this cheese.
Sniff!

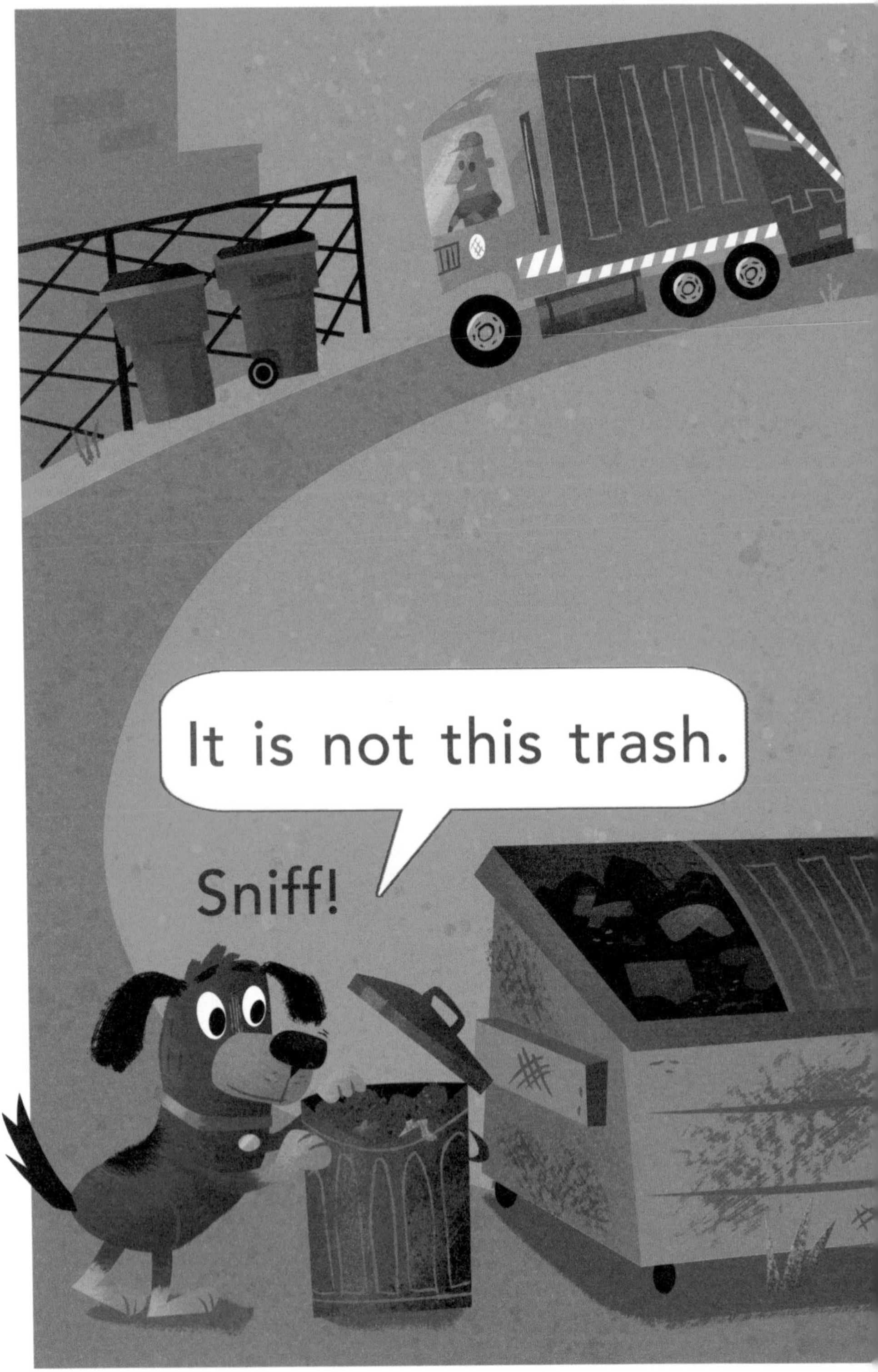
It is not this trash.
Sniff!

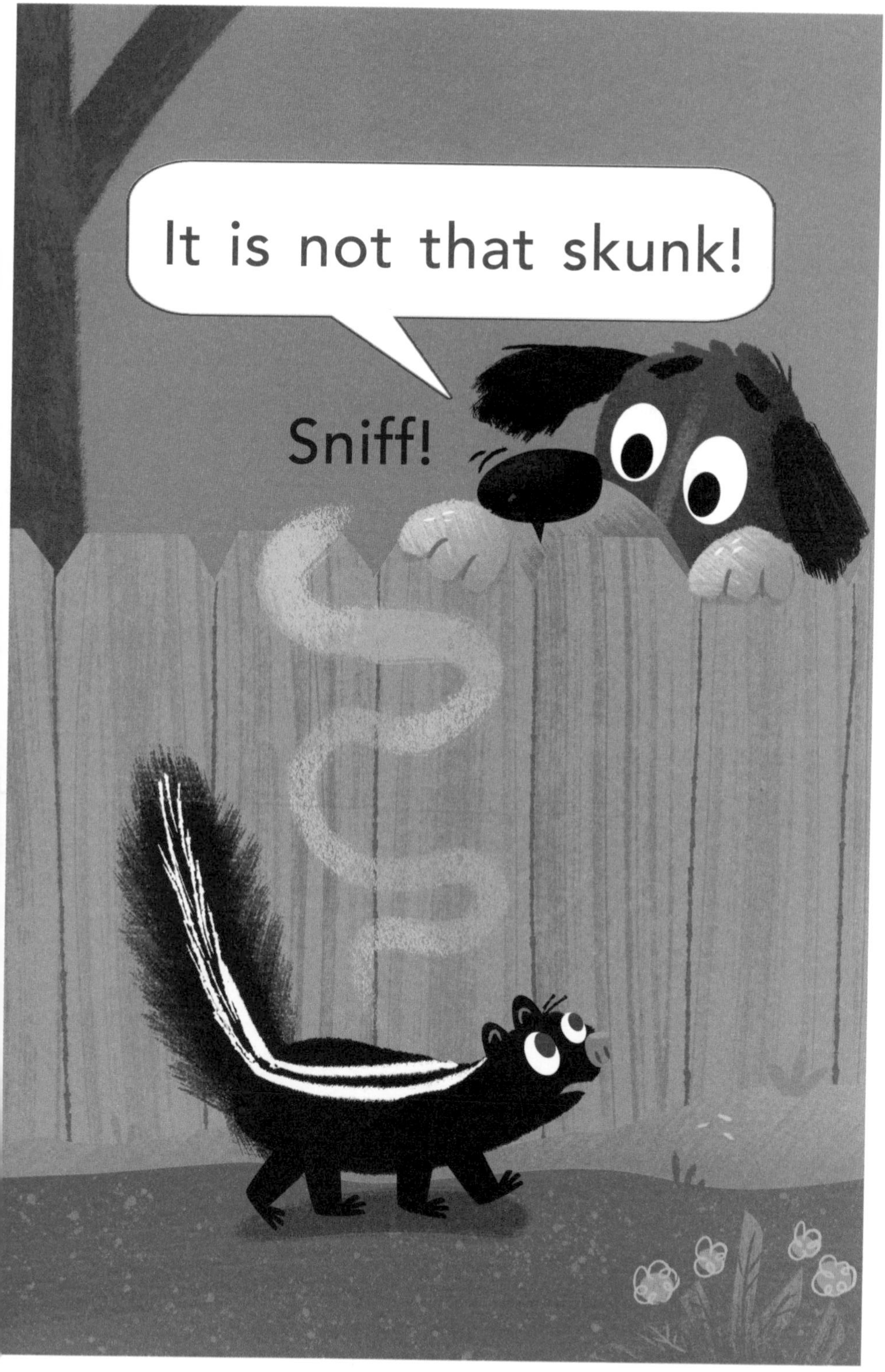
It is not that skunk!
Sniff!

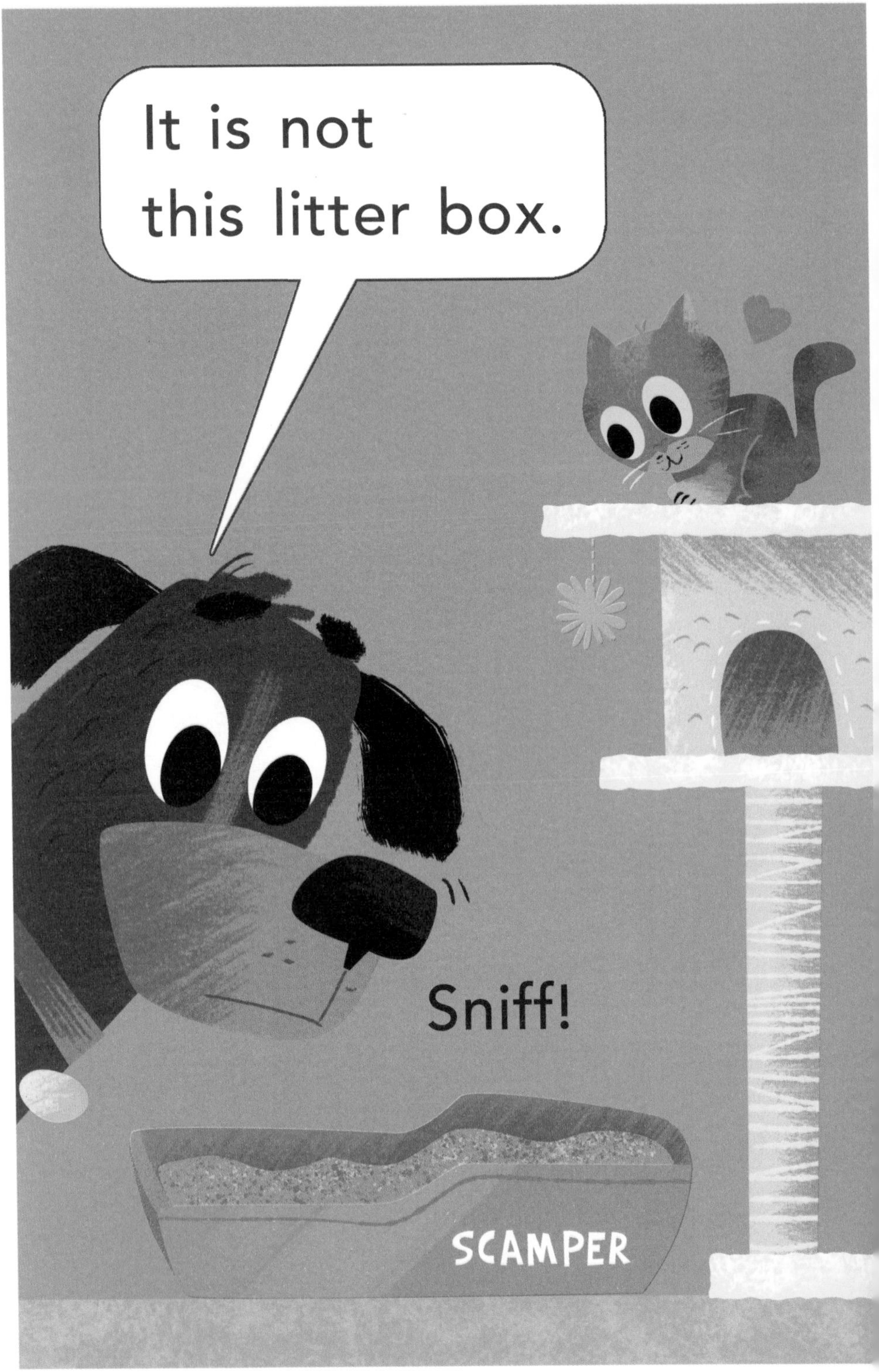
It is not
this litter box.
Sniff!
SCAMPER

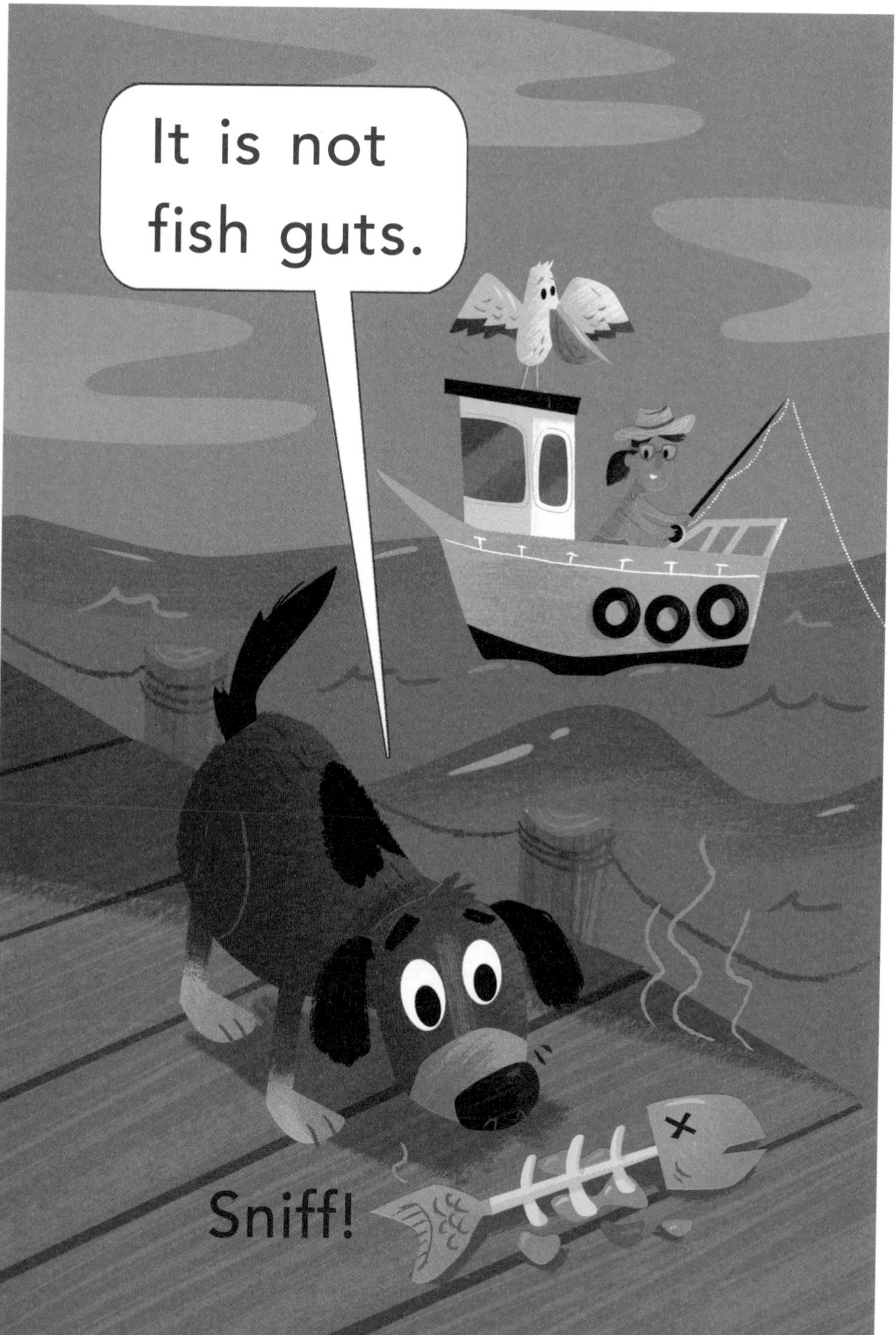
It is not
fish guts.
Sniff!

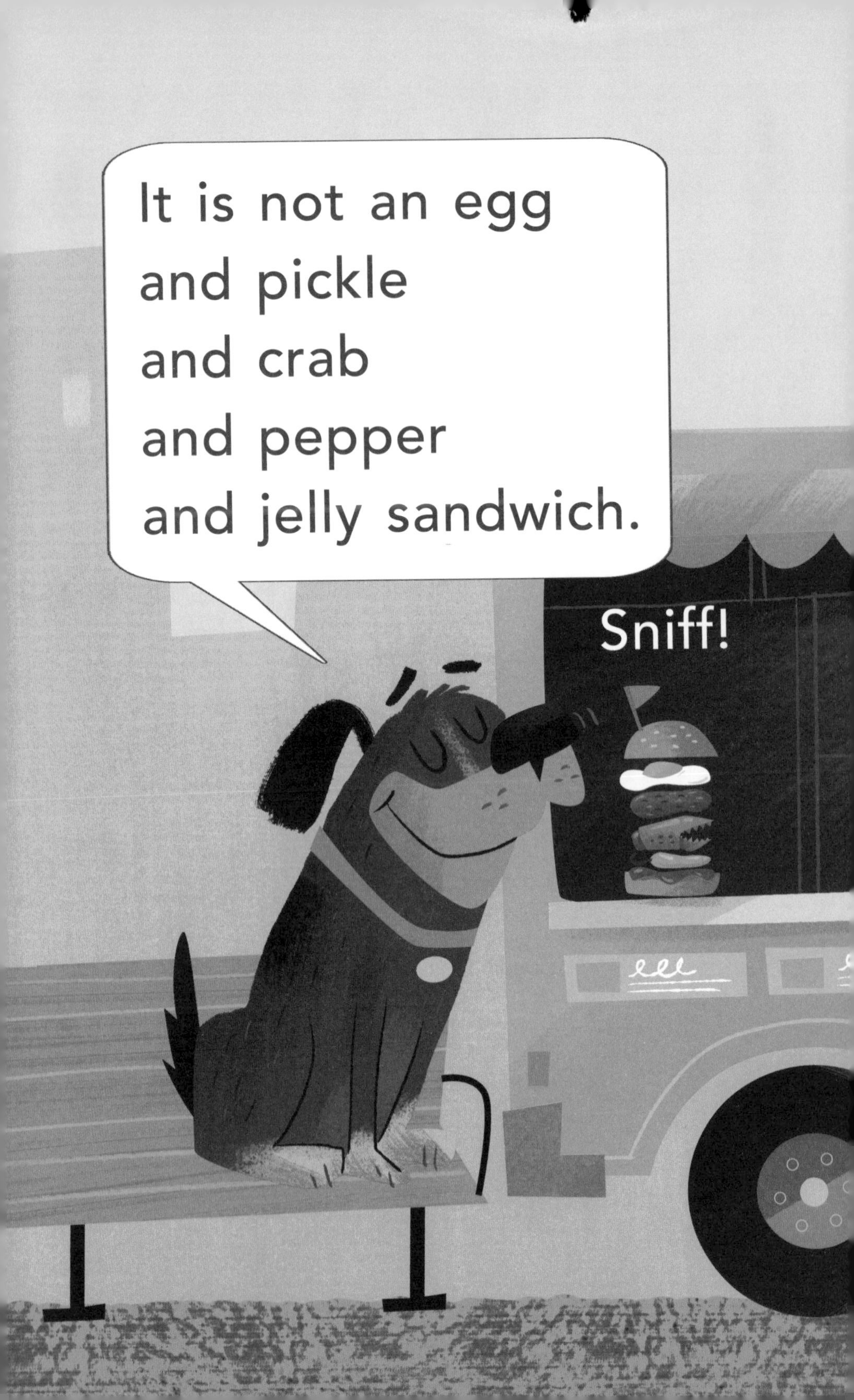
It is not an egg
and pickle
and crab
and pepper
and jelly sandwich.
Sniff!

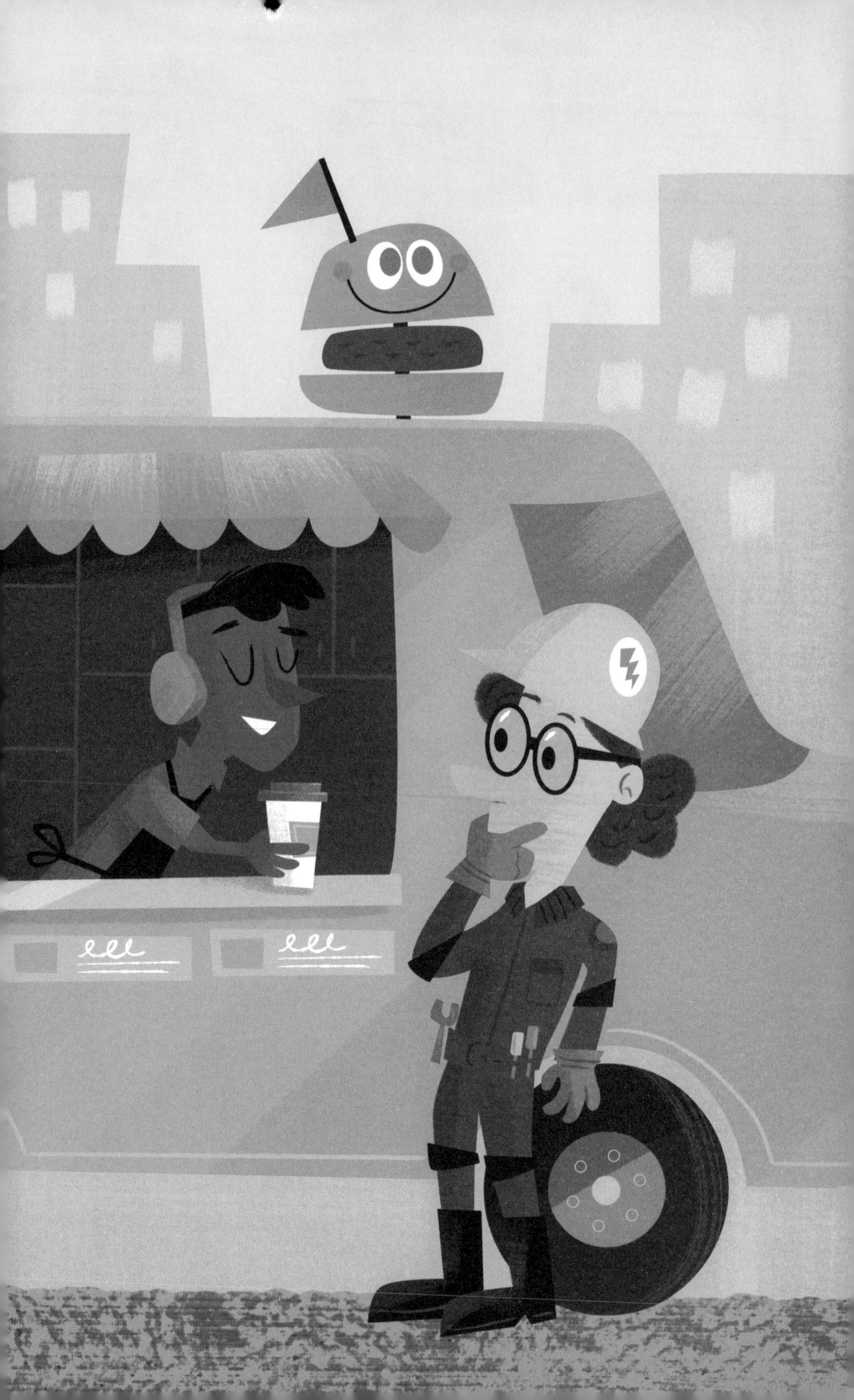

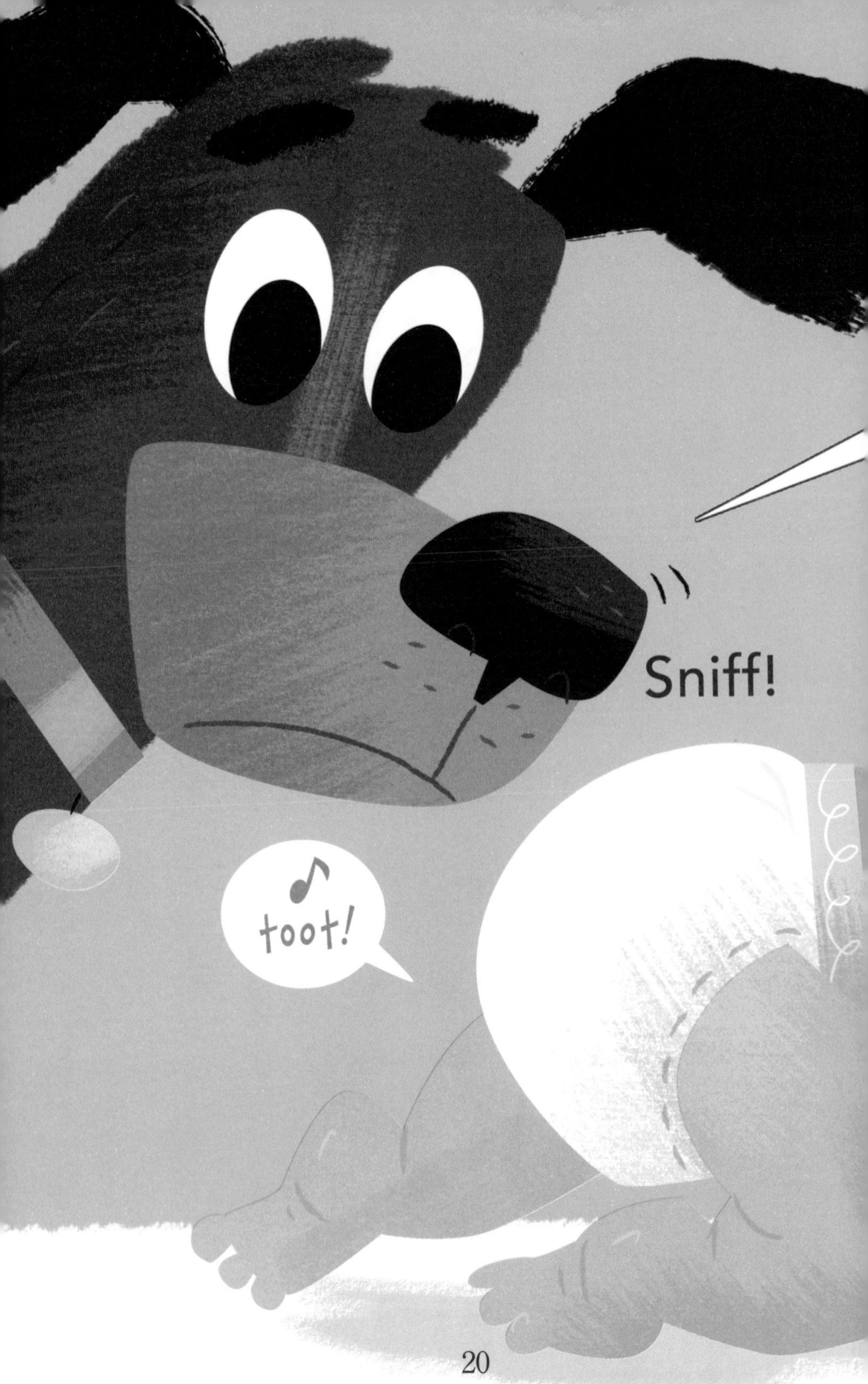
Sniff!
toot!

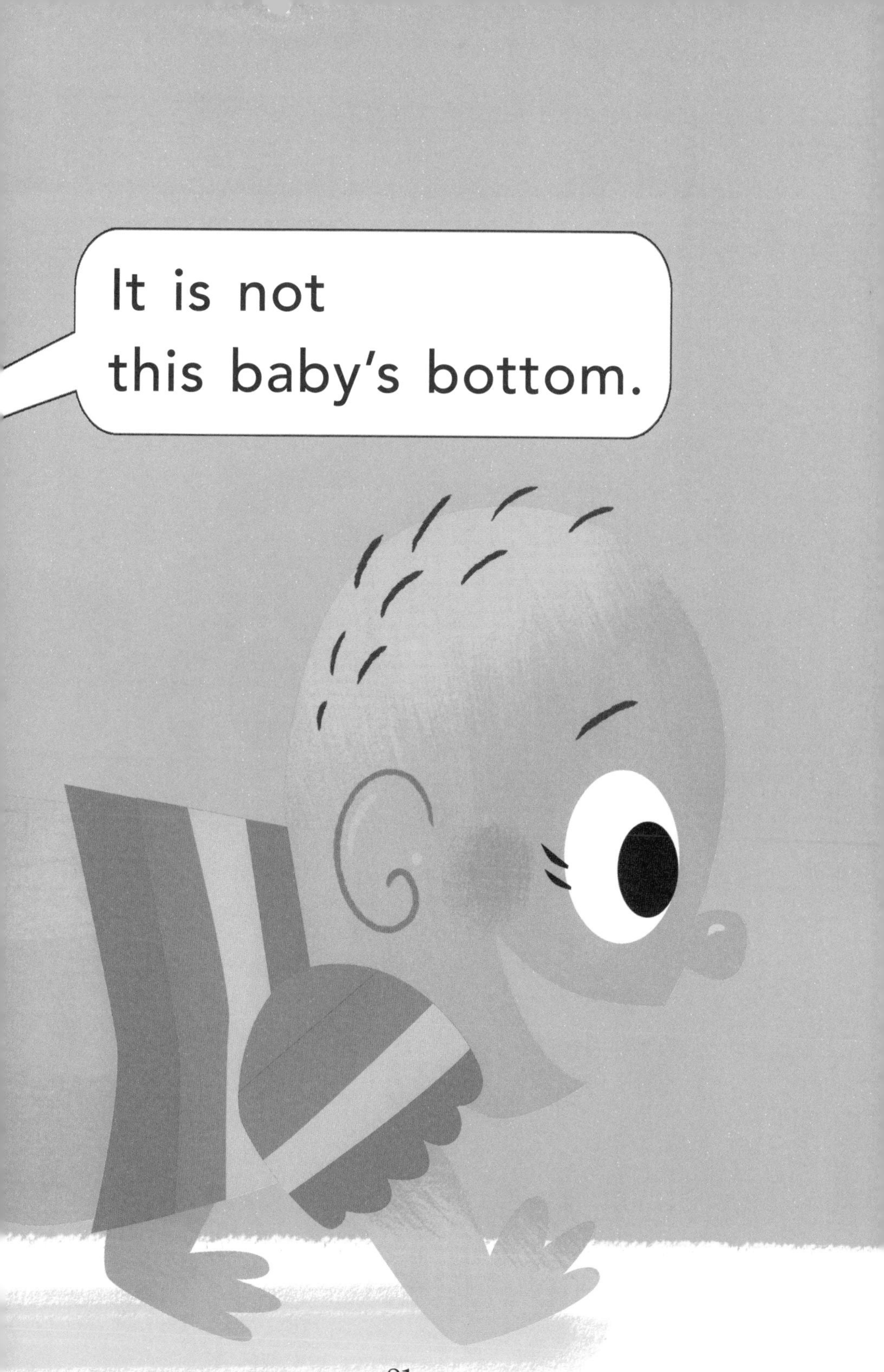
It is not
this baby's bottom.

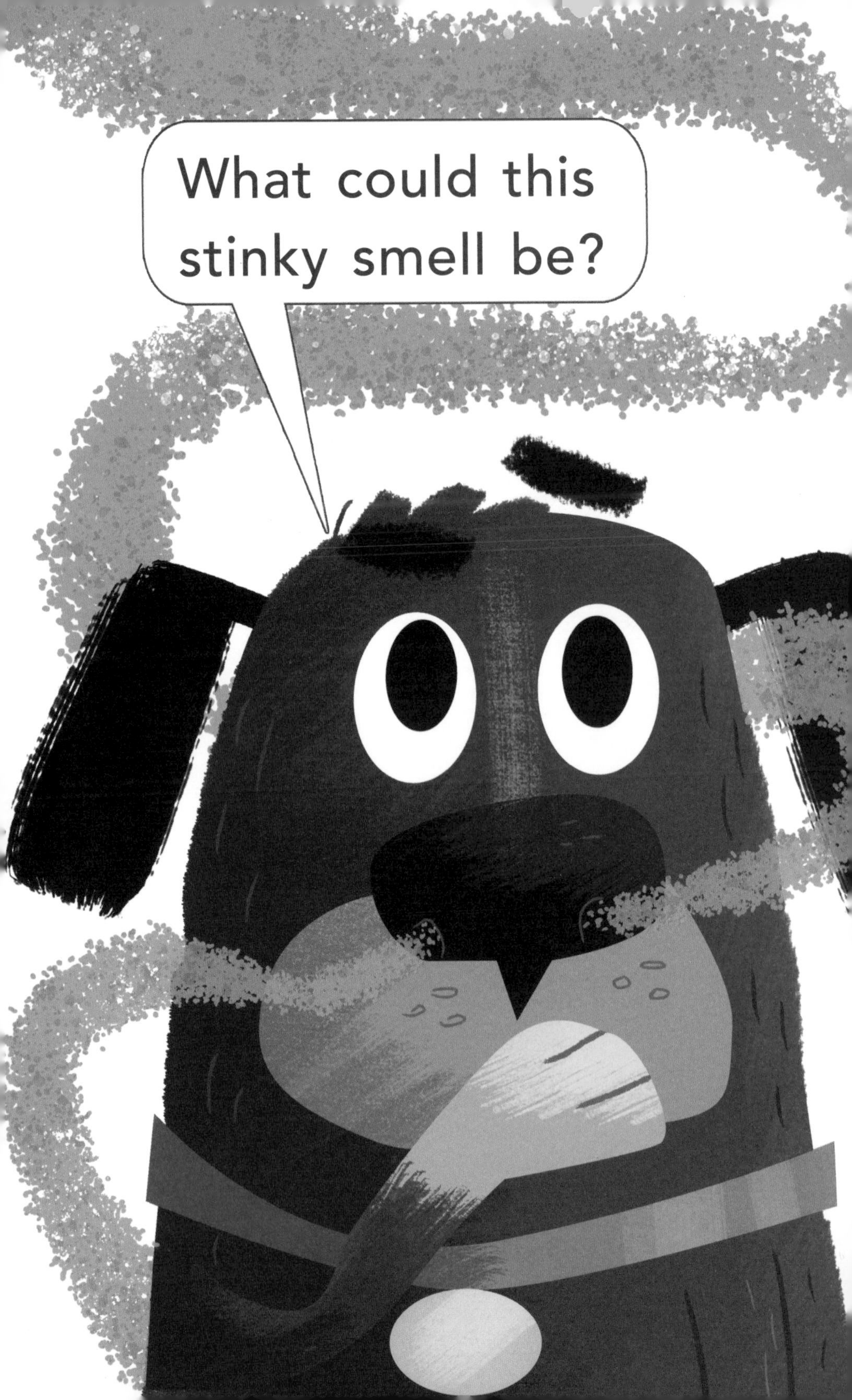
What could this stinky smell be?

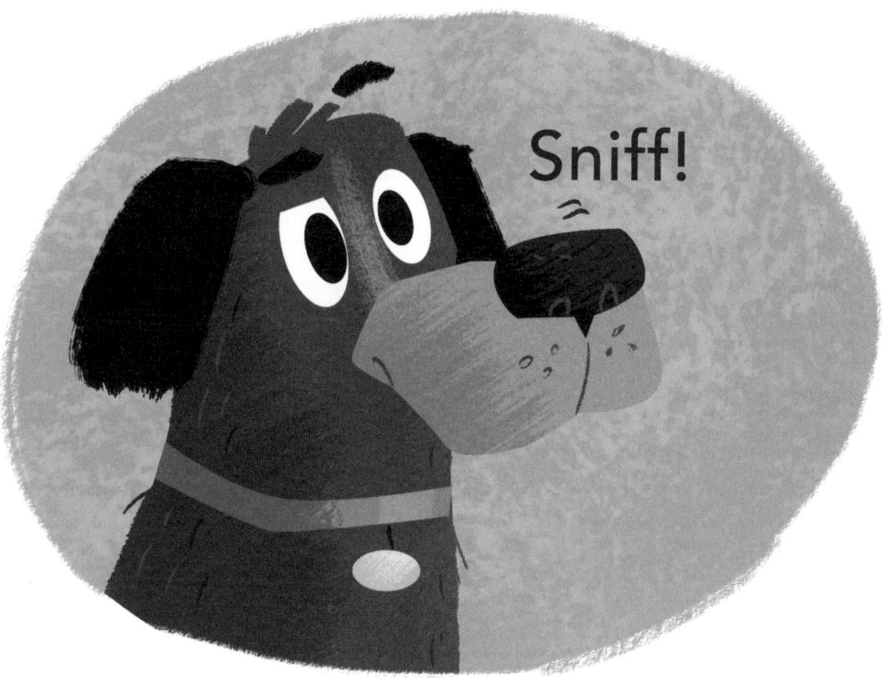
Sniff!

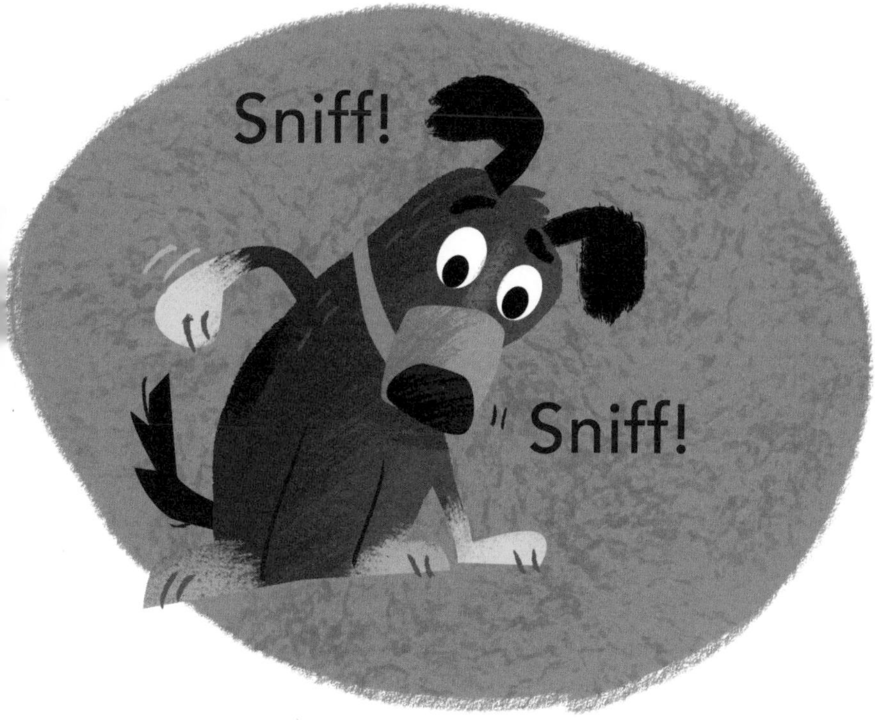
Sniff!
Sniff!

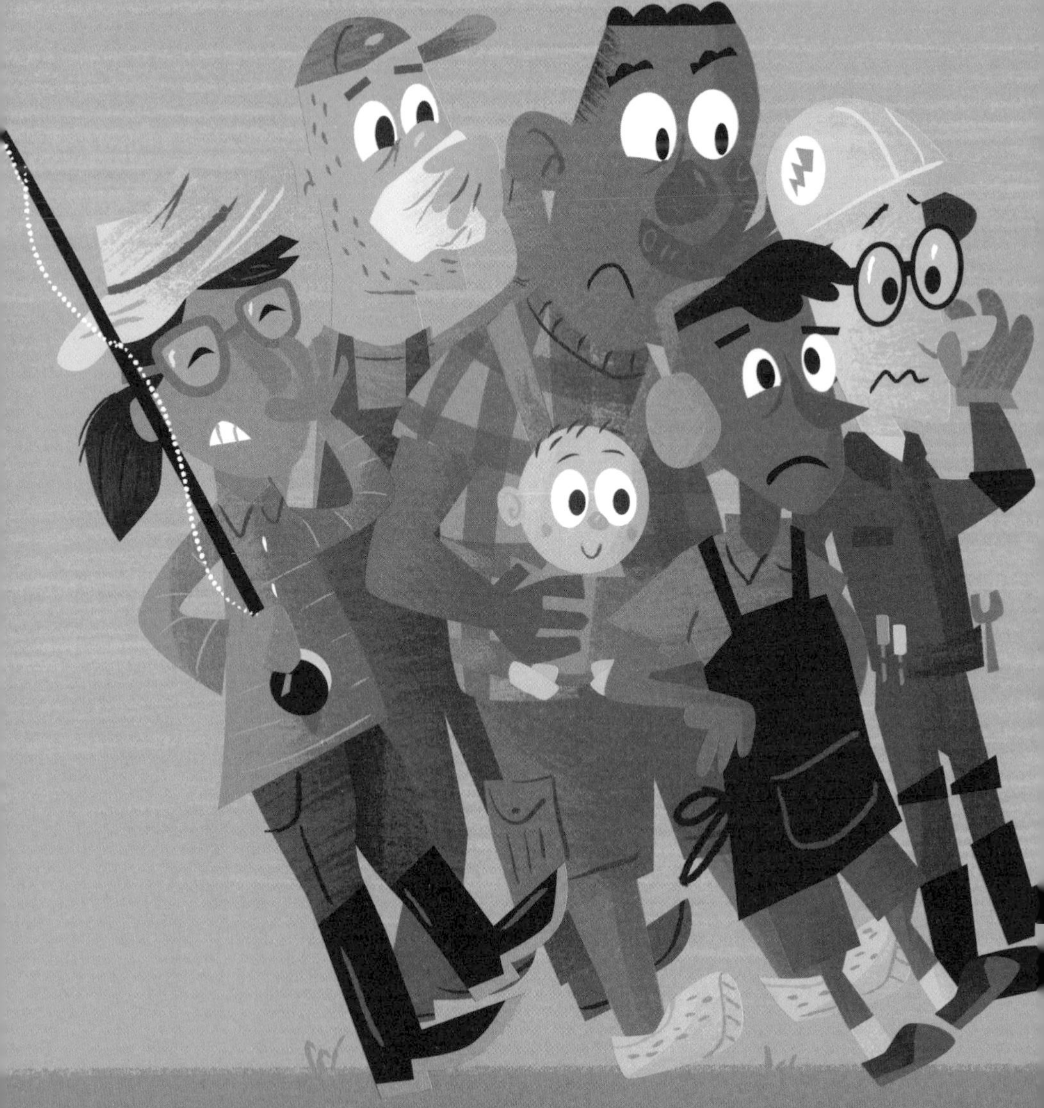

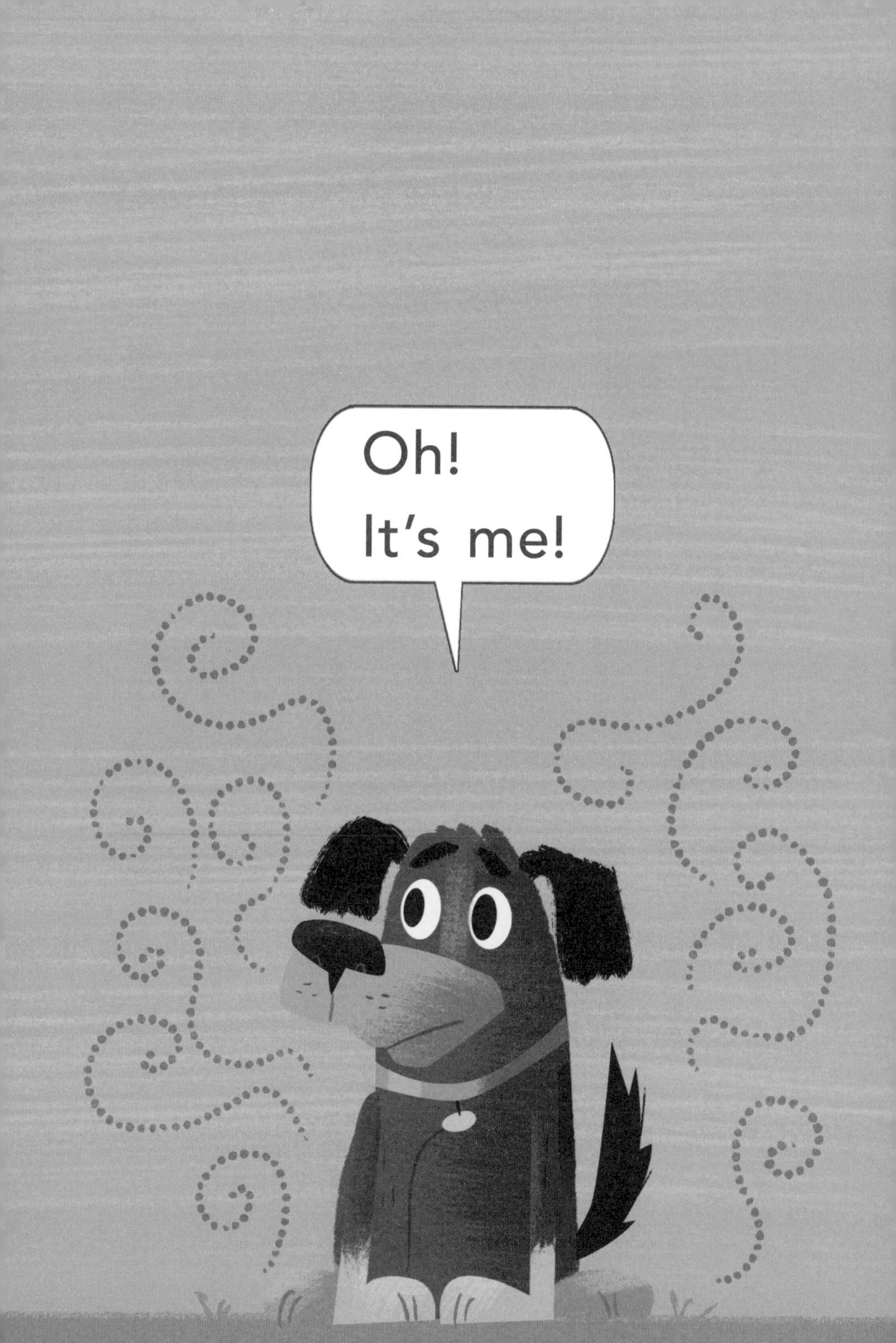
Oh!
It's me!

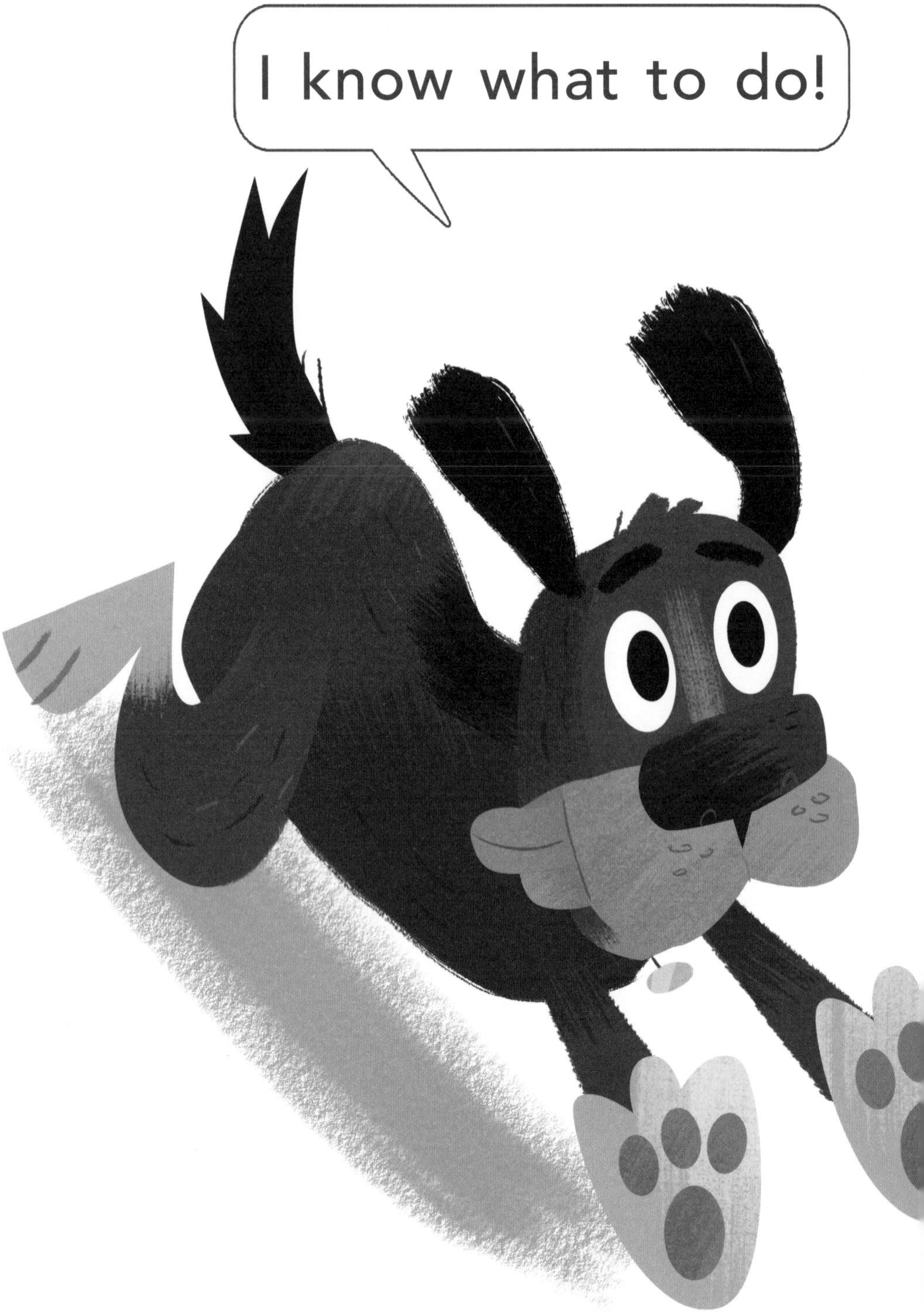
I know what to do!

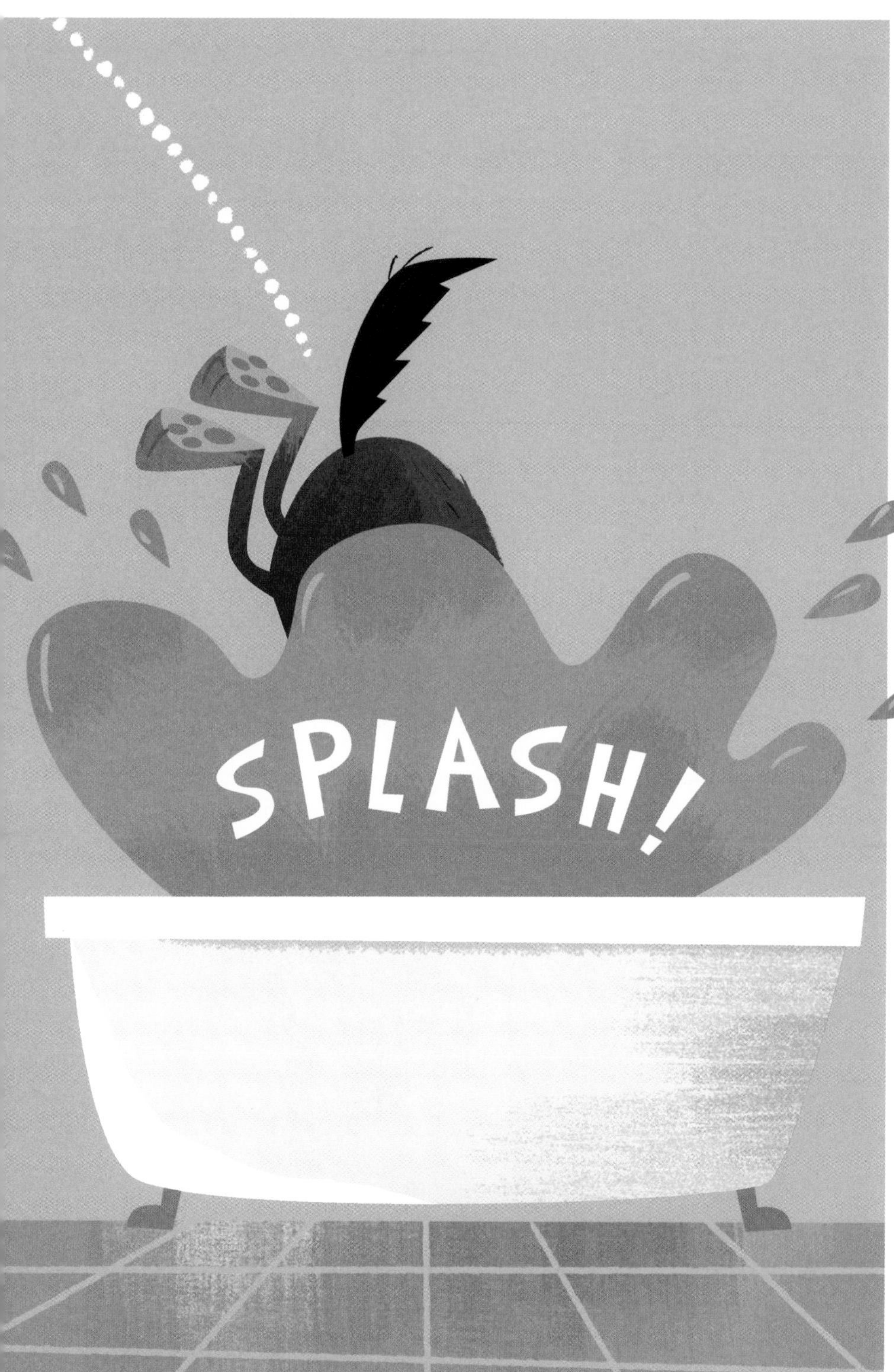
SPLASH!

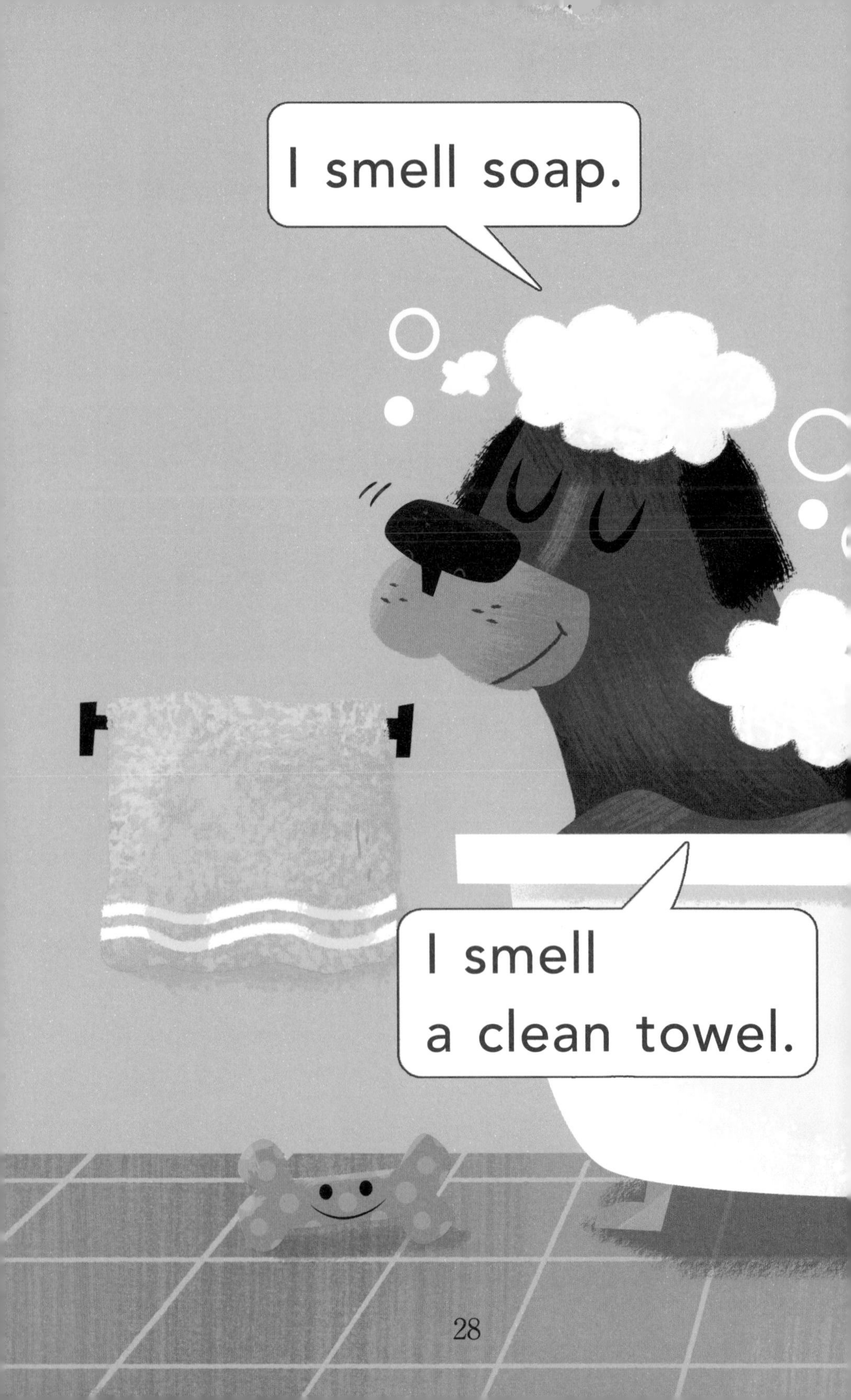
I smell soap.
I smell a clean towel.

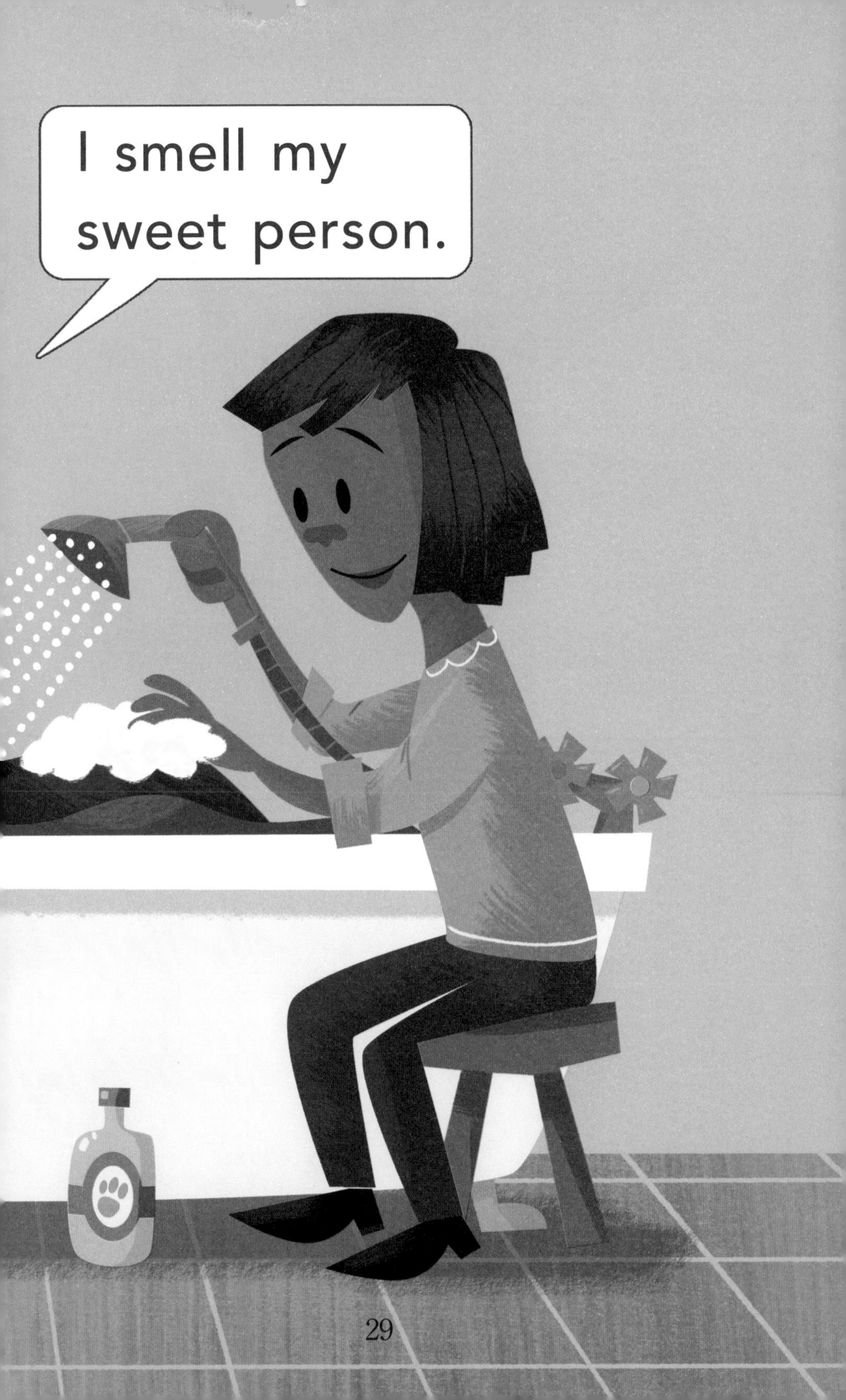
I smell my sweet person.

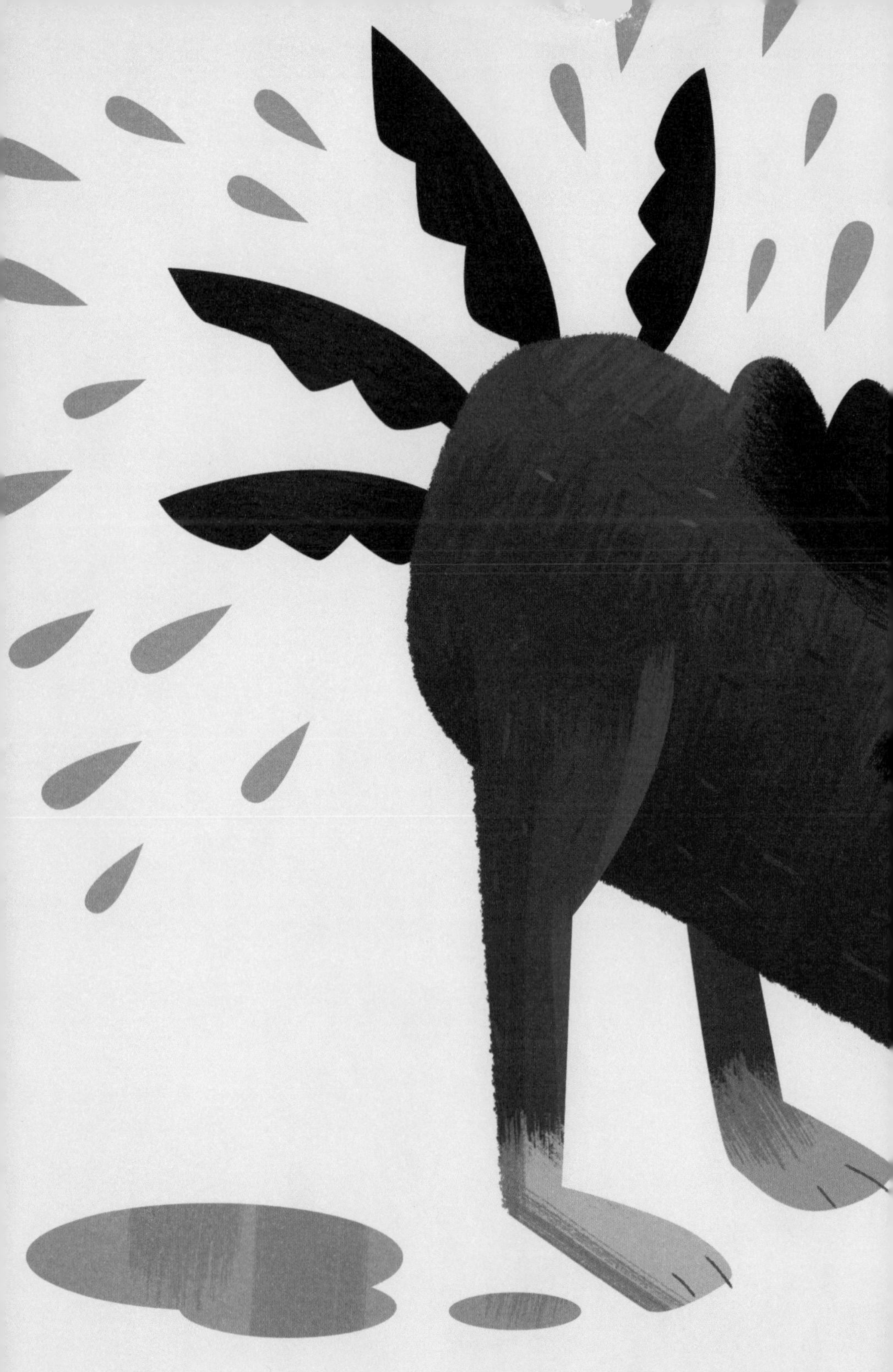

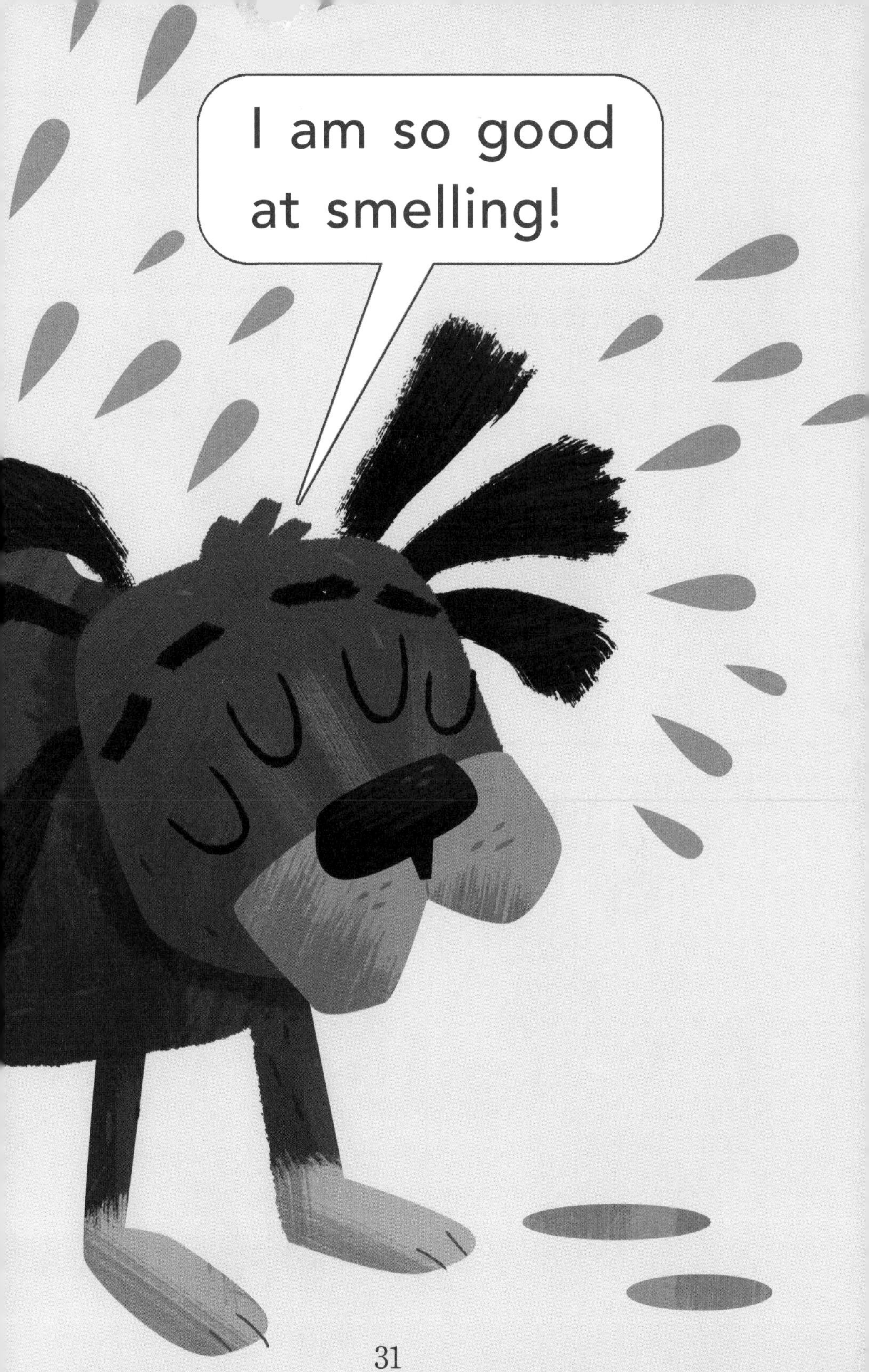
I am so good
at smelling!

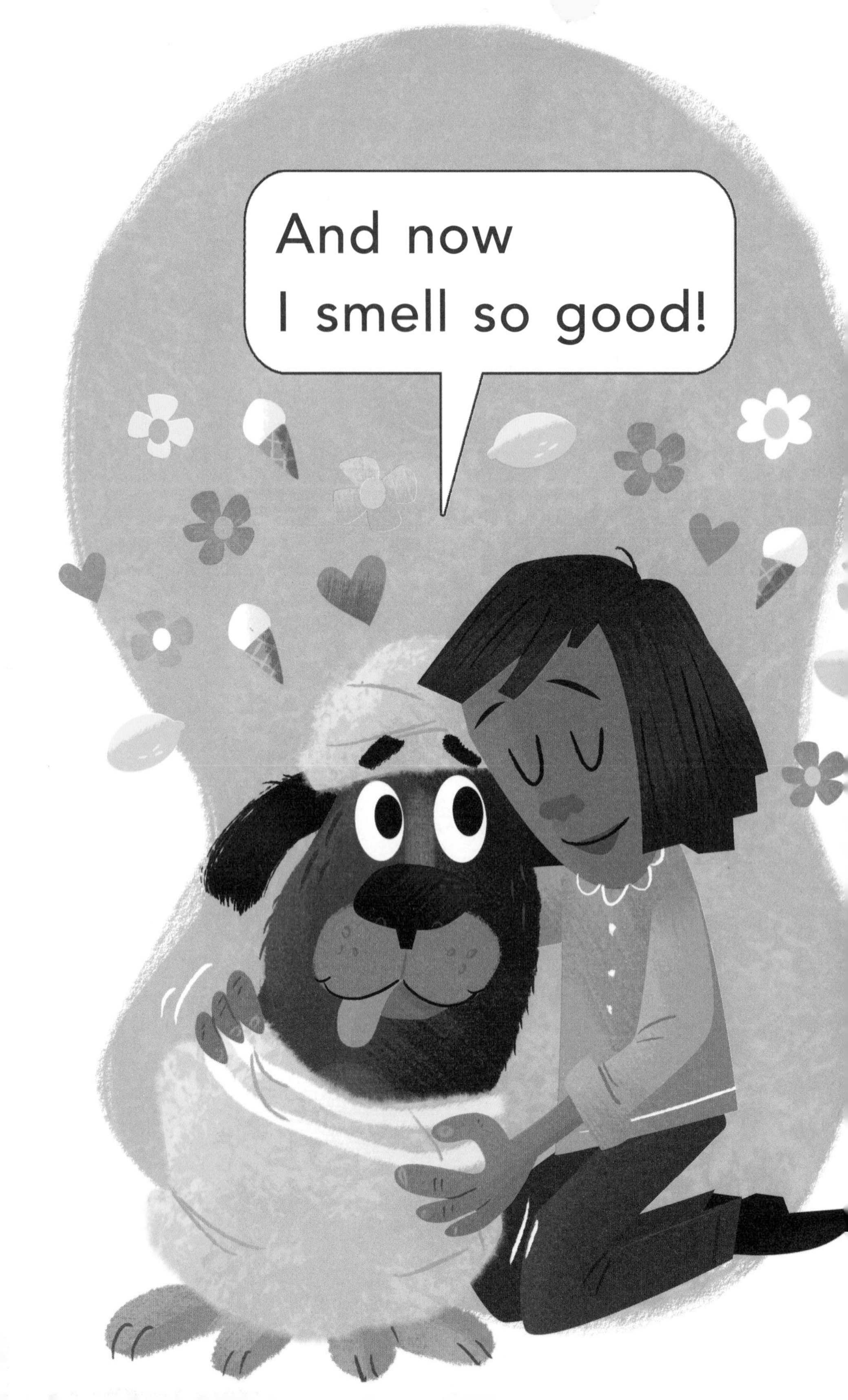
And now I smell so good!